THE WORKS OF

HENRY VAN DYKE

AVALON EDITION

VOLUME XIII

ᵉ

INDOOR ESSAYS

III

Avalon

Henry van Dyke's home in Princeton

IDEALS
AND APPLICATIONS

BY

HENRY VAN DYKE

NEW YORK

CHARLES SCRIBNER'S SONS

1921

To

MY FRIEND AND COLLEAGUE
CHARLES WILLIAM KENNEDY
WITH WHOM I HAVE HAD JOY IN WORK
AT PRINCETON

PREFACE

THE forces that reside in temperament give strength to action. The ideals that guide it are in the mind and heart.

A man moves slowly or swiftly, he does his work weakly or strongly, according to the amount of vital energy that is in him. But the direction of his life, this way or that way, follows the unseen influence of what he admires and loves and believes in.

It is not easy to take stock of these controlling ideals. It is harder still to arrange them in a clear, logical, consistent philosophy of life. Few men have the ability to make such a total statement of their spiritual assets. Even for those who might be able to do it after a fashion, it is difficult to find the time, because they are actively engaged in the business of living.

But every now and then a man is asked to write or to speak on some occasion, or about some question, that calls him to consider some of his ideals in relation to the matter in hand. It is not always possible, nor often necessary, to give a full description of his point of view, or to trace the paths of inheritance or reasoning by which he has reached it. What he has to do is just to stand where he belongs, to be loyal to his faith, and to apply his ideals to the question before him.

That which is spoken or written in this way may have some interest as showing the practical conclusions to which certain principles lead. And if, as I believe, life is the test of thought, rather than thought the test of life, we should be able to get light on the real value of a man's ideals and beliefs, by looking at the effect which they would have in human conduct if they were faithfully applied.

It is in this way that the chapters of this book have been written, and thus I would beg the reader to take them. They were addresses or special articles prepared for certain occasions. They were not born of theory but of practical experience. I have tried to approach certain points in education, in politics, in literature, in religion, in the conduct of life, from the stand-point of one who wishes to be guided in every-day judgments and affairs by a sane idealism. The book is not a defence, nor even a statement, of a complete system of philosophy or faith. It is simply a collection of essays in application.

CONTENTS

ON POLITICS
AND POLITETHICS

I

IS THE WORLD GROWING BETTER?*

NO man knows, of a certainty, the answer to this question.

If it were an inquiry into the condition of the world's pocket-book, or farm, or garden, or machine-house, or library, or school-room, the answer would be easy. Six million more spindles whirling in the world's workshops in 1903 than in 1900; eight hundred million more bushels of wheat in the world's grain-fields than in 1897; an average school-attendance gaining 145 per cent between 1840 and 1888, while the population of Europe increased only 33 per cent: thus the figures run in every department. No doubt the world is busier, richer, better fed, and probably it knows more, than ever before.

I am not one of those highly ethereal and supercilious people who can find nothing in this to please them, and who cry lackadaisically: "What is all this worth?" I am honest enough to confess to a sense of satisfaction when my little vegetable garden rewards my care with

* *Everybody's Magazine*, December, 1904.

an enlarged crop, or when my children bring home a good report from school. Why should not a common-sense philanthropy lead us to feel in the same way about the improved condition and the better reports of the big world to which we belong?

To be sure, our satisfaction is checked and shadowed, often very darkly shadowed, by the remembrance of those who are left behind in the march of civilization—the retarded races, the benighted classes, the poor relations of the world. But our sympathy with them is much more likely to be helpful if it is hopeful, than if it is despairing. I do not think it necessary to cultivate melancholy or misanthropy as a preparation for beneficence.

A generous man ought to find something cheerful and encouraging to his own labours in the knowledge that the world is growing *better off*.

But is it growing *better?* That is another question, and a far more important one. What is happening to the world itself, the owner of all this gear, the prosperous old adventurer whose wealth, according to Mr. Gladstone, increased twice as much during the first seventy years of the nineteenth century as it had done during the eighteen hundred years preceding?

IS THE WORLD GROWING BETTER?

Is this marvellous increase of goods beneficial to the character of the race? Or is it injurious? Or has it, perhaps, no deep or definite influence one way or the other?

You know how hard it is to come to a clear and just conclusion on such points as these, even in the case of an individual man. Peter Silvergilt's wealth has grown from nothing to three hundred million dollars during the last fifty years; but are you sure that Peter's personality is better, finer, nobler, more admirable than it was when he was an errand-boy earning ten dollars a week? William Wiseman has a world-wide fame as a scholar; it is commonly reported that he has forgotten more than most men ever knew; but can you trust William more implicitly to be fair and true and generous than when he was an obscure student just beginning to work for a degree in philosophy?

When we try to apply such questions, not to a single person, but to the world at large, positive and mathematical answers are impossible. The field of inquiry is too vast. The facts of racial character are too secret and subtle.

But a provisional estimate of the general condition of the world from the point of view of goodness, comparing the present with the past —a probable guess at the direction in which the race is moving morally—this is something that we may fairly make. Indeed, if you think and care much about your brother men you can hardly help making it, and upon the colour of this guess the tone of your philosophy depends. If the colour is dark, you belong among the pessimists, who cannot be very happy, though they are sometimes very useful. If the colour is bright, you are what men call an optimist, though I think Doctor John Brown's word "meliorist," would be a more fitting name.

For what is it, after all, that we can venture to claim for this old world of ours, at most? Certainly not that it is altogether good, nor even that it is as good as it might be and therefore ought to be. Police-stations and prisons and wars are confessions that some things are wrong and need correction. The largest claim that a cheerful man who is also a thoughtful man—a child of hope with his eyes open—dares to make for the world is that it is better than it used to be, and that it has a fair prospect of further improvement. This is meliorism, the philosophy of actual and possible betterment; not a high-stepping, trumpet-blowing, self-flattering creed, immediately available for advertising purposes; but a modest and sober faith, useful for consolation in those hours of despon-

dency and personal disappointment when the
grasshopper and the critic both become a burden, and for encouragement to more earnest
effort in those hours of cheer when a high-tide
of the spirit fills us with good-will to our fellow-
men.

I asked John Friendly the other day: "Do
you think the world is growing better?"

"Certainly," said he, with a smile like sun-
rise on his honest face, "I haven't the slightest
doubt of it."

"But what makes you so sure of it?"

"Why, it must be so! Look at all the work
that is being done to-day to educate people and
help them into better ways of living. All this
effort must count for something. The wagon
must move with so many horses pulling at it.
The world can't help growing better!"

Then he left me, to go down to a meeting of
his "Citizens' Committee for the Application of
the Social Boycott to Political Offenders" (which
frequently adjourns without a quorum). Immediately afterward I passed the door of the
"Michael T. Moriarty Republicratic Club"—
wide open and crowded. On my way up Sixth
Avenue I saw a liquor-saloon on every block—
and all busy. The news-stands were full of
placards announcing articles in the magazines—

IDEALS AND APPLICATIONS

"Graft in Chicago," "The Criminal Calendar of Millionaires," "St. Louis, the Bribers' Paradise," "The Plunder of Philadelphia." Headlines in the yellow journals told of "Immense Slaughter in Manchuria," "Russia Ripe for Revolution," "The Black Hand Terror in the Bronx," "Gilded Gambling-Dens of the Four Hundred," "Diamonds and Divorce."

John Friendly's cheerful *a priori* confidence in the betterment of the world seemed to need reinforcement. Some of the horses are pulling his way, no doubt, but a good many appear to be pulling the other way. Under such conditions the wagon may stick fast, or go backward. Possibly it may be pulled to pieces. Who can measure, in the abstract, the comparative strength of the good and the evil forces? Who can tell beforehand which way the tug-of-war must go?

The only sound and satisfactory method is to bring out the foot-rule of fact and apply it to the tracks of the wagon. Has it moved? How fast, how far, which way?

But first of all we must get a clear notion of what we mean by growing better. It is a phrase about which a company of college professors would probably have a long preliminary dispute; but plain people understand it well enough for practical purposes. There are three factors in it. When we say that a man grows better, we mean that, in the main, he is becoming more just, and careful to do the right thing; more kind, and ready to do the helpful thing; more self-controlled, and willing to sacrifice his personal will to the general welfare. Is the world growing better in this sense? Is there more justice, more kindness, more self-control among the inhabitants of earth than in the days of old?

Of course, when we consider a question like this, before even a modest guess at the answer is possible, we must be willing to take a long view and a wide view. The world, like the individual man, has its moods and its vagaries, its cold fits and its hot fits, its backslidings and its repentances, its reactions and its revivals. An advance made in one century may be partly lost in the next, and regained with interest in a later century. One nation may be degenerating, under local infections of evil, while others are improving. There may be years, or regions, of short harvest in the field of morals, just as there are in the cotton-field or the corn-field. The same general conditions that work well for the development of most men, may prove unfavourable to certain races.

9

IDEALS AND APPLICATIONS

Civilization seems to oppress and demoralize some tribes to the point of extinction.

Liberty is a tonic too strong for certain temperaments; it intoxicates them.

But what we have to look at is not the local exception, nor the temporary reaction: it is the broad field as far as we can see it, the general movement as far as we can trace it. And as I try to look at the question in this way, clearly and steadily, it seems to me that the world is really growing better: not in every eddy, but in the main current of its life; not in a straight line, but with a winding course; not in every respect, but in at least two of the three main points of goodness; not swiftly, but slowly, surely, really growing better.

Take the matter of justice. The world's sense of equity, its desire to act fairly and render to every man his due, is expressed most directly in its laws. Who can fail to see a process of improvement in the spirit and temper of legislation, a conscientious effort to make the law more efficient in the protection of human rights and more just in the punishment of offences?

In Shakespeare's time, for example, a woman's existence, in the eye of the law, was merged in that of her husband. A man could say of his wife: "She is my goods, my chattels; she is my house, my household stuff, my field, my barn, my horse, my ox, my anything." The very presents which he gave her were still his property. He could beat her. He could deprive her of the guardianship of her children. It was not until the end of the seventeenth century that the law secured her right to the separate use of her property, and not until the middle of the nineteenth century that the legislation of Great Britain and America began to recognise and protect her as a *persona*, entitled to work and receive wages, to dispose of her own earnings, to have an equal share with her husband in the guardianship of their children. Surely it is an immense gain in justice that a woman should be treated as a human person.

This gain is most evident, of course, in those nations which are leading the march of civilization. But I think we can see traces of it elsewhere. The abolition of child-marriage and the practical extinction of the *suttee* in India, the decline of the cruelly significant fashion of "foot-binding" in China, the beginning of the education of girls in Egypt, are hints that even the heathen world is learning to believe that woman may have a claim to justice.

In the same way we must interpret the laws

for the protection of the young against cruelty, oppression, and injustice. Beginning with the Factory Act of 1833 and the Mines and Collieries Act of 1842 in England, there has been a steadily increasing effort to diminish and prevent the degradation of the race by the enslavement of childhood to labour. Even the parent's right of control, says the modern world, must be held in harmony with the child's right to life and growth, mental, moral, and physical. The law itself must recognise the injustice of dealing with young delinquents as if they were old and hardened criminals. Let us have no more herding of children ten and twelve years old in the common jail! Juvenile courts and probation officers, asylums and reformatories: an intelligent and systematic effort to reclaim the young life before it has fallen into hopeless bondage to crime: this is the spirit of civilized legislation to-day. In 1903 no less than ten of the American States enacted special statutes with this end in view.

The great change for the better in modern criminal law is another proof that the world is growing more just. Brutal and degrading methods of execution, such as crucifixion, burying alive, impaling, disembowelling, breaking on the wheel: the judicial torture of prisoners and unwilling witnesses by the thumb-screw, the strappado, and the rack: cruel and agonising penalties of various kinds have been abolished, not merely by way of concession to humanity, but with the purpose of maintaining justice in purity and dignity.

The world has been learning to discriminate more carefully between the degrees of crime. In the eighteenth century men were condemned to the death penalty for forgery; for stealing from a shop to the value of five shillings or from a house to the value of forty shillings; for malicious injury to trees, cattle, or fish-ponds; for the cutting of hop-bands from the poles in a plantation. Within eighty years capital punishment has been inflicted in England for sheep-stealing and for robbery from a house. The laws of Pennsylvania at the time of the Revolution enumerated twenty crimes punishable with death; in Virginia and Kentucky there were twenty-seven. Modern legislation recognises the futility as well as the fundamental injustice of such crass and indiscriminate retribution, and reserves the death penalty for a supreme crime against the life of the individual or the State.

At the same time there has been a twofold rectification of the scope of the criminal law. Some of the offences most severely punished in

13

old times have ceased to be grounds of prosecution at all: for example, heresy, witchcraft, religious nonconformity. On the other hand, misdeeds which formerly were disregarded have been made punishable. It was not until 1833 that the English law began to treat drunkenness as a misdemeanour, rather than a misfortune. In 1857 a fraud on the part of a trustee, and in 1875 the falsification of accounts, were declared to be criminal. The laws of various States are recognising and defining a vast number of new misdemeanours, such as the adulteration of foods, gambling, violation of laws in restraint of the liquor traffic, selling cigarettes to children, tapping electric wires, disfiguring the landscape with advertisements or printing them on the American flag, making combinations in restraint of trade, sleeping in a public bakery, spitting on the floor of a street-car. I do not say that all of these offences are wisely defined or fairly punished; but I do say that the process of modern legislation in regard to such matters indicates a growing desire among men that justice shall prevail in the community.

A large part of what appears to be the increase of crime in recent years (according to statistics), is due to this new definition. There are more offenders in the most peaceful and well-governed States, because there are more offences defined. Another part comes from the greater efficiency in the execution of laws and the greater completeness in the tabulation of reports. The remaining part comes from a cause on which I will touch later. But in spite of this apparent increase of crime, no sensible man believes that the actual amount of violence and disorder among men is as great as it used to be. Pike's "History of Crime in England" estimates that in the fourteenth century murders were at least sixteen times as frequent as in our own day.

I pass by such notorious and splendid triumphs of the world's moral sense as the abolition of the slave-trade, and the recognition of international law, to mention two small, concrete illustrations of what I mean by the advance of justice. The purchase by the American Government of the lands of the Spanish friars in the Philippines was a just way of accomplishing what would have been done a century ago by confiscation. The passage by the Congress of the United States of an act granting to foreigners copyright in their literary works, was a recognition, resisted by selfishness and ignorance for fifty years, of the fundamental principles of righteousness and fair dealing.

I know there are many items, and some of

15

them most grievous, to be set down on the other side. There are still wars of conquest; corruptions and delays in legislation; oppressions and inequalities in government; robberies and cruelties which go unpunished.

But these are not new things: they are as old as sin; evils not yet shaken off. I do not dream that the world is already quite just. But by the light that comes from the wiser, fairer laws of many lands, I reckon that the world is growing more just.

In regard to the increase of kindness in the human race, the evidence is even more clear and strong. There are more people in the world who love mercy, and they are having better success in making their spirit prevail. More is being done to-day to prevent and mitigate human suffering, to shelter and protect the weak and helpless, to minister wisely to the sick and wounded in body and in mind, than ever before in the history of mankind. Part of the evidence of this lies in some of the facts already noted in connection with the humanizing of the law, and in the extraordinary story of the work begun by John Howard, a hundred and thirty years ago, which has cleansed away at least a part of the shame of a cruel, filthy, and irrational prison-system. But there is evidence, also, of a more direct and positive sort, going beyond the removal of ancient evils and manifesting a spirit of creative kindness eager to find new ways of helping others.

Since the middle of the nineteenth century, says the best authority on statistics, charity has grown twice as fast as wealth in England, three times as fast in France. In the United States the annual amount of the larger gifts ($5,000 or more) rose from $29,000,000, in 1893, to $107,-000,000, in 1901. The public and private charities of New York alone (excluding the money spent on buildings) are estimated at $50,000,000 a year.

With all this increase of money comes an equal increase of care and thought in regard to the best way of using it for the real benefit of mankind. Reckless almsgiving is recognised as an amiable but idiotic form of self-indulgence.

The penny dropped into the beggar's hat gives place to an inquiry into the beggar's condition. This costs more, but it is worth more. Waste in money given is no more virtuous than waste in money earned. Schools of philanthropy are established to study and teach the economics of generosity. Asylums are investigated and supervised. Relief funds are intrusted to responsible committees, who keep books and render accounts. Men and women are trying to take the head into partnership with the heart in beneficence. A rich father and mother lose their child by scarlet fever: they give a million dollars to endow an institution for the study and prevention of infectious diseases. An excursion steamboat is burned in New York harbor and a thousand people, most of them poor, lose their lives: within two weeks $125,000 is given for relief; it is not thrown away with open hands, but administered by a committee with as much care as they would bestow on their own affairs; every dollar is accounted for, and a balance of $17,000 is left, to meet future calls, or to be devoted to some kindred purpose. These are illustrations of intelligent mercy.

Consider the advance in the general spirit of kindness which is indicated by the founding and successful operation of a system of Working Men's Insurance. Incidentally there has been an immense benefit in the increase of precautions to prevent accidents and to reduce dangerous occupations. The employer who is not yet willing to protect his workmen for kindness' sake, will do it to escape heavier taxes. And the community which silently compels him to do this, the community which says to the labouring man, "If you will perform your duty, you shall not starve when you are sick and old," is certainly growing more kind as well as more just.

Look at the broad field of what we may call international mercy. It has been estimated that since the days when the failure of the harvest drove Abraham from Palestine down to Egypt to seek food for his starving people, there have been three hundred and fifty great famines in various parts of the world. How many of the hungry nations received help from the outside world before the nineteenth century began? But now, within a week after the distress is known, money, food, and help of all kinds begin to flow in from all quarters of the globe. The famine in India in 1900–1901 called forth contributions from Great Britain, Germany, France, America, to the amount of $72,000,000. The greater part came from England, of course, but the whole world stood ready to aid her.

After the great fire of London in 1666, and the Lisbon earthquake in 1755, there was some outside assistance given, it is true. But in the main, the stricken cities had to suffer alone and help themselves. When the little American city of Galveston, Texas, was swept by flood in 1900, within three weeks $750,000 was poured in for its relief, and the whole fund amounted to nearly a million and a half.

Turn again to look at the effort which the world is making to get rid of the hell of war, or, if that be not possible, at least to mitigate its horrors and torments. The High Tribunal of Arbitration at The Hague is a milestone on the world's path of progress toward the peaceful method of solving international disputes. Each year sees some new advance in that direction. Recently Great Britain and France, Holland and Denmark, France and Spain, Great Britain and Italy, France and Holland, Great Britain and Spain, Italy and France, have made treaties by which they pledge themselves to refer all differences of certain kinds which may arise between them to this tribunal for settlement. During the same time at least seven international questions have been referred to special arbitrators.

True, war has not yet been eliminated from the programme of the race. Great armaments are maintained at incredible expense, and nations insist, as Ruskin said, that it is good policy to purchase terror of one another at the cost of hundreds of millions every year. Some of the honest friends of peace are not yet reasonable enough to see the folly of this arrangement.

IS THE WORLD GROWING BETTER?

A peace which depends only upon fear is nothing but a suppressed war. Every now and then the restraining fear gives way, in one place or another, and hundreds of thousands of men are dressed in uniform and marshalled with music to blow one another's brains out.

But, in spite of all this, the growth of the spirit of mercy in the world makes itself known in the application of more humane rules to the inhumanity of war. Private wars, prevalent in the Middle Ages, and piracy, tolerated until the nineteenth century, have been practically abolished. The slaughter, torture, and enslavement of prisoners of war, which was formerly practised even by Christian nations, gave place in the middle of the seventeenth century to the custom of releasing all prisoners at the close of the war without ransom. Even Mahometan nations agreed by treaty that they would no longer subject their captives to bondage or torture. Persia and Turkey, in 1828, pledged themselves to the exchange of prisoners.

There has been a steady advance in the strictness and efficiency of the rules protecting the life and property of non-combatants, an immense decrease in the atrocities inflicted by conquering armies upon the peaceful inhabitants

21

of vanquished countries. Let any man read the story of the siege and sack of a town in Holland by the Spanish soldiers as it is given in Motley's *Dutch Republic*, and compare it with the story of the capture of Paris in 1870, or even the taking of Pekin in 1900, and he will understand that war itself has felt to some extent the restraining touch of mercy. Let him reflect upon the significance of the work of the Red Cross Society, with its pledge of kindly succour to all who are wounded in battle, "treating friend and foe alike"; let him consider the remarkable fact that in Japan this society has a service as perfectly organised as any in the world, with a million members, and an annual income of more than $1,500,000, and he cannot but acknowledge that the spirit of pity and compassion has gained ground since the days of Charlemagne and Barbarossa and Napoleon—yes, even since the days of Libby Prison and Elmira Prison.

If none of these things are enough to comfort or encourage him, let him take in the meaning of the simple fact that not one of the great nations of the world to-day would dare to proclaim a war *in the name of Religion*. By this change alone, I should make bold to guess that the world is surely growing better.

But how is it with the third factor of real

betterment: self-restraint, the willingness to sacrifice one's own passion and pleasure for the good of others? Here, I confess, my guessing is confused and troubled. There was a vast improvement from the fourteenth to the nineteenth century, no doubt. But whether the twentieth century is carrying on the advance seems uncertain.

It may be that on this point we have entered into a period of reaction. The theory of emotional self-realization threatens to assert itself in dangerous forms. Literature and art are throwing their enchantments about the old lie that life's highest value is found in moments of intense self-gratification. Speed is glorified, regardless of direction. Strength is worshipped at the expense of reason. Success is deified as the power to do what one likes. Gilding covers a multitude of sins.

On the one hand, we have a so-called "upper class," which says: "The world was made to amuse me; nothing else matters." On the other hand, we have an apparent increase of the "criminal class," which lives at war with the social order. Corporations and labour unions engage in struggles so fierce that the rights and interests of the community are forgotten by both parties. In our own country lynching, which is organised murder for unproved offences, grows more common; divorces increase to sixty thousand in one year; and there is an epidemic of shocking accidents and disasters, greater than any hitherto recorded, and due apparently to the spirit of unrestraint and recklessness which is sweeping furiously in its motor-car along the highways of modern life.

Is this selfish and headlong spirit growing? Will it continue to accelerate the pace at which men live, and diminish the self-control by which they are guided? Will it weaken more and more the bonds of reverence, and mutual consideration, and household fidelity, and civic virtue, until the states which have been civilized by the sanctions of love and the convictions of duty are whirled backward, by the passion of self-indulgence, into the barbarism of luxurious pleasure or the anarchy of social strife?

These are the questions that rise to trouble us in our moments of despondency and foreboding. But I think that it is neither wise nor brave to give them an answer of despair. Two are stronger than one. The growth of justice and of kindness, I guess, will in the long run prevail over the decline of self-restraint, and the selfish, reckless spirit will be overcome.

At all events, when Christmas comes I shall sit down with John Friendly to enjoy its cheer, rather than with any sour pessimist. One thing is sure. The hope of humanity lies in the widening, deepening influence of that blessed Life which was born nineteen hundred years ago in Bethlehem. The Lesson which that Life teaches us is that the sure way to make the world better is for each man to do his best.

Christmas, 1904.

THE GREAT RELAPSE

Christmas, 1920! Sixteen years have passed since the foregoing pages were written. Between then and now what dread disaster has befallen our too cheerful hopes, what hideous war-clouds have shadowed the world and drenched it with blood and tears!

Whence came this tempest of wrath? Out of the depths of human nature, not yet delivered from the lusts and passions that war within us and make wars around us: out of the reckless greed of our civilization centering its efforts on material riches and luxury and neglecting the discipline of the mind and heart: and especially out of the violent "will to power" of the German Empire, ready to set fire to the world in order to gain its dominion. These

were the sources of the vast world-war of 1914–
1918, whose after-flames still burn along the
borders and whose ashes cover the face of the
earth.

How immense the cost of that conflagration!
Eight million human lives swiftly blotted out
in battle, and as many more slowly devoured
by misery and heart-break, disease and starvation; two hundred billion dollars' worth of
world-wealth squandered in destruction or desperately spent in defence; fair cities and famous
temples laid in ruin, fertile lands left bare and
desolate; the health of the race impaired by
pestilence and famine; the mind of millions
poisoned by wild hatreds, shaken by swift tu-
mults of unrest, shell-shocked into a state of dull
suspicion, anxious fear, and sudden anger that
comes near insanity,—what a frightful price
mankind has had to pay! And for what? For
nothing, absolutely nothing; unless,—*unless indeed it was for liberty and a lesson.* Liberty to
begin again, trying to make the world better:
the lesson that it never can be done until to a
clearer ideal of justice and a deeper impulse
of mercy, mankind shall join a greater power
of self-control.

That was the point at which the slow progress
of the race,—a real advance by small degrees,

though far from perfection,—that was the point where the process of peaceful development broke down in 1914, and the world was plunged into the awful pit of strife and the red mire of slaughter. I was wrong in saying that "two are stronger than one." My calculation that because the sense of justice and the motive of kindness were increasing all must go well, was too hasty, too easy, too absolute. At a given hour, for a certain time, one may be stronger than two.

> "*Yet all these fences and their whole array*
> *One cunning bosom-sin blows quite away.*"

It was the lack of self-control in German ambition, it was the reckless and ruthless urge of self-aggrandisement and the lust of mondial dominion, that swept away the restraints of righteousness and silenced the scruples of compassion and made Germany will war to win world-power. "Upon the heads of her diplomats and princes are the blood and guilt of it." But the burden and the sorrow and the calamity of it press heavily upon all the nations.

Yet in our dejection and the revulsion of our minds, in our shock of dismay that such a thing could happen in the Twentieth Century, we must beware of falling into the dark exaggera-

tions of despair. This latest war was indeed
the largest, but I do not believe that it was
the most terrible, cruel, and barbarous known
to history. Let us be sane in our judgments
and seek not to claim a false pre-eminence for
our own time even in evil things. Much of
what mankind had gained through the cen-
turies in mitigation of the concomitant horrors
of warfare was forfeited to the Teutonic theory
of *Schrecklichkeit*, and the Allies themselves
were not free from reproach in their methods
of reprisal. Poison-gas, submarines, aerial bom-
bardments are indiscriminate and horrible weapons. But after all there were some things in
ancient warfare which were not practised, for
very shame, in this great conflict of arms.

Prisoners of war were not chained in the gal-
leys, nor decapitated by thousands. Wicked
things were done in Louvain and Dinant and
Lille and elsewhere. But rich captured cities
were not given over to death and destruction.
When Sulla took Athens the massacre of the
inhabitants was so fierce that the blood filled
the market-place like a pool and ran out of the
city gate. When Titus destroyed Jerusalem,
when the Goths sacked Rome, nothing was
spared. When "The Spanish Fury" fell on
Antwerp in 1576, eight thousand people were

murdered in three days. Nothing comparable
with that happened in Belgium or Northern
France in the late war. It was bad, unspeak-
ably bad, but it was not as bad as in the olden
time. If it had been, half the population of
Europe would have perished.

International law, though often broken and
evaded by the Germans, was never wholly
denied. They even promised to make good
their transgressions when they had won their
victory! The blackest page of the whole history was the massacre of the Armenians by
the Turks,—the unforgettable crime of an un-
pardonable despotism.

Through all this long and ghastly strife the
Red Cross went calmly and bravely on its er-
rands of mercy to friend and foe, ministering to
the sick and wounded, seeking with a divine inconsistency to help with one hand of civilization
those whom the other hand had smitten down.

Nor may we forget, amid our natural abhorrence of the repulsive realities of war, that there
was a real and essential difference between the
two sides in the combat. Germany was the
actual assailant, she attacked, she invaded,
fighting for the extension of her empire, for
"a place in the sun," which she claimed as needful for her fuller self-realization. The Allies

were on the defensive. They fought on their own soil to maintain their liberties, their rights, their honour, and their life.

Now it is profoundly unreasonable to ignore the vital difference between these two kinds of war, and so to put them on a level, either in the same honour or in the same condemnation. Even those who hold the absolute pacifist theory that physical resistance to evil is never permissible, must still admit that the aggressor has a far deeper guilt than the man who withstands aggression. On the other hand, we who believe that the gift of strength carries an obligation to use it for the protection of assaulted virtue, imperilled freedom, and justice endangered or openly attacked, must hold that men who take arms in such a cause are soldiers of the right, "thrice-armed" because they "have their quarrel just." Believing this, I regard the victory of the Allies and America in the late war as in the main, (and despite all minor draw-backs and delinquencies,) a great moral victory and a proof that the world *is* growing better. If anyone doubts this let him consider the alternative; let him read the programmes which the Lords of Potsdam issued before and during their mad adventure; let him think carefully what the triumph of the

German Empire would have meant to the rest of mankind. Seeing that this great disaster did not come to pass, let us thank God and take courage.

But these considerations are only rays of light gilding the cloud of danger, distress, and apprehension that still hangs over us. Will the world ever be much better unless we get rid of the anachronism of war as the arbiter of disputes between nations? May not this method of violence and unreason at any moment thrust us back from the path of progress, destroy our dearly bought gains of justice and mercy, and, overthrowing the shaken pillars of civilization, bring back upon the world the dark and shelterless night of barbarism?

Undoubtedly it may, and probably it will, unless men of good-will unite their efforts everywhere, and work together to prevent war and to establish peace on strong foundations.

Two things will certainly help the wounded world to recover from its great relapse and move forward again on the path of progress. First, we must make a clear and definite endeavour to bring a regulative, disciplinary influence into the processes of education. We must try to bring up a new generation to understand and respect, not only the sanctity of jus-

tice and the beauty of human-kindness, but also
the necessity of self-control. This work can
only be done through individuals, in the home,
the school, the church. It must be plain and
patient, watchful and sympathetic, loving and
uncompromising, satisfied with nothing less than
the creation of a finer, stronger, more self-re-
strained man,—

"King of himself and servant of mankind."

Such men will do their best to avoid and avert
war.

Second, we must carry the principle of self-
control, (which is so essential in the social relations of the community that we protect and
uphold it by law,) into the international relations of the world. We must learn to think of
national sovereignty in terms of self-restraint
as well as in terms of action. We must inter-
pose every possible barrier between the cold
ambition of rulers, or the hot passions of the
multitude, and those aggressive policies and
deeds which thrust war upon an unwilling world.
We must devise practical means by which the
cause of countries aggrieved or injured may
have a prompt appeal to an impartial council
of arbitration, or a fair and speedy trial before
a high court of international law.

IS THE WORLD GROWING BETTER?

But, you say, we already have those things, at least in outline. Well then, all that we need is to make them work, and to put behind them the combined force, the concerted powers of those free nations that believe in justice, mercy, and self-control as the vital elements of human progress.

In this good hope we labour. We believe that the world has grown better. We confess that it has suffered, apparently, after the weariness of a great trial the discouragement of a great relapse. *But we set our will and our work towards a great recovery, in which the world shall grow better yet.*

II

RULING CLASSES IN A DEMOCRACY*

A DEMOCRACY differs from a monarchy, an empire, an oligarchy, not in the absence of ruling classes, but in the method by which they are selected.

Government without rulers is as impossible as steering without rudders. Man is by nature a civil creature. His natural rights, however you may define them, coexist with a natural instinct of organisation. Organisation implies order. Order implies control. Control implies authority. Authority implies a ruling class.

Rudiments of this civil instinct may be seen in some of the lower animals. Bees and ants reflect, in a dim and partial way, the image of an organised state. Herds of elephants and horses, colonies of birds and beavers, are obedient to leadership and direction. In almost every case we can measure a creature's place in the scale of intelligence by the force and efficiency of the civil instinct. Man is no exception, but the great example. The first social problem is

* Centennial Address, University of Georgia, June 19, 1901.

34

the problem of rule: who shall exercise it, how far shall it go, and by what means shall it be enforced? The highest social triumph is the establishment of authority in the hands of those who are best fitted to exercise it.

But while man has an instinct which recognises and seeks this end, he has also an impulse which rebels against the means necessary to secure it. The freedom of the will carries with it the craving for unrestrained liberty of action. But liberty absolutely unrestrained is inconsistent with the existence of any kind of social order.

Suppose that you and I are farmers, whose fields march together. If you are free to do just what you please, and I am free to do precisely what I like, it is not probable that peace will prevail along our line-fences; at least, not until we are both perfectly sanctified and the millennium arrives, which is evidently some distance away. Meantime it is quite necessary for both of us that there should be some one authorised and competent to say what shall be done about those line-fences; and how the roads which we use in common shall be kept up; and how the agreements which we make to exchange our labour, or the products of our labour, shall be enforced; and what means shall be used to

35

guard us both against common dangers and disasters; and how the cost of these things shall be divided.

This is rule. The men who have "the say" about these subjects belong to the ruling classes. Against them, and against the things that they say, the impulse of unregulated freedom always reluctates.

Few men doubt their ability to make laws. Most men, at some time or other, dislike the necessity of obeying them. Personal restraints are not often personal pleasures. The visit of the tax-collector seldom gives unmixed joy. It is easier to do what you please than to do what you ought. Individual rights seem more concrete and familiar than reciprocal duties. Under every form of government known to man there has been, there still is, and there probably always will be, an element of discontent and restlessness arising from the natural human impulse—natural at least to man in his present condition—to resist rule.

The problem of civilization is how to subdue this impulse by correlating individual rights with social duties, and how to develop, enlighten, and guide the civil instinct which seeks order through rule.

Now, it is evident that the method of selecting the ruling classes must have a considerable influence in the working out of this problem. It is true that at any given time people are most likely to be contented, peaceful, and happy under the rulers who actually give them the most firm, orderly, and equitable government, no matter how they may have been selected. There is a certain amount of hard common sense in the remark of Alexander Pope, although it was made in verse:

> "*For forms of government let fools contest*
> *Whate'er is best administered is best.*"

But the wisdom of this couplet is confined to the present tense. It is good only for the moment in which it is uttered. A form of government may be well administered to-day, badly to-morrow. The great question is, how to secure a continuity of good administration. How shall the men who are best qualified to control and direct the common interests of their fellow-men be discovered? How shall they be sanctioned in the use of just authority, and restrained from the exercise of unjust tyranny? How shall it be made most easy to correct the accident of power falling into unfit hands? How shall the great force of public opinion, from which, in the last analysis, all governments de-

rive their energy and stability—how shall this
common sense of justice and right be satisfied in
the selection of the ruling class?

Different methods have been devised. They
may be classed under three heads: autocratic,
automatic, and democratic.

The autocratic method practically amounts
to allowing the chief ruler to select himself
and appoint his subordinates. This is the oldest
method and the rudest—

> *"the simple plan*
> *That those should take who have the power,*
> *And those should keep who can."*

It is based upon the assumption that might
coincides with right. This would be convenient
if it were true. It would be a great saving of
time if we could just let the strongest man rule,
and feel sure that he was the best. But, unfor-
tunately, the history of imperial sway does not
support this idea. When an autocrat imposes
the taxes, there is often "the de'il to pay."
And when a tyrant chooses the judges, Justice
does not need to have her eyes bandaged, for
she is stone-blind already.

The automatic method relies upon heredity
to supply the ruling classes. Certain families
are endowed with titles and powers, and the

head of a particular family inherits the sovereignty. All that he has to do is to be born at the right time, and live long enough, and the sceptre comes to him as a matter of course. Meantime natural forces are at work producing hereditary legislators to support and share his power. The scheme has an aspect of antique dignity and piety. It appears to put great reliance upon Providence, and, indeed, it has often sanctioned itself in old times by an appeal to the "Divine Right of Kings." In practice it has two very serious drawbacks. First, the wrong family may be chosen to start the procession; and, second, the so-called law of heredity often produces very unexpected and curious results.

The democratic method intrusts the selection of the ruling classes to the collective reason and justice of the people. In the conduct of government it appeals to the governed for their consent. "Consent of the governed," in this connection, does not mean their submission, merely; for if this were the meaning, it would be equally true of a constitutional monarchy, and even of a benevolent and popular empire. The subjects of reasonable and just monarchs "consent," in this sense, to their governments, with practically as much unanimity as the citizens of the United States feel at any given time in consenting to the authority of the President in office. The consent of democracy, if it has any distinctive meaning, must signify the thinking together, the acting together,(*consensio,*) of the people in the choice of their rulers, and, consequently, in the direction of the state. Three things are essential to the reality of this popular participation.

First, there must be an untrammelled opportunity for the people to express their choice by suffrage. It is by no means necessary that this suffrage should be universal. As a matter of fact, it never has been. There is no nation known to history in which all the people, male and female, old and young, native and foreign-born, have had the suffrage. It is not a common right. It is a civil privilege intended to protect common rights. It has always been restricted in one way or another. The only things necessary to its sufficiency are that it should be truly representative, and that the conditions which restrict it should be equal for all, except in the case of forfeiture for crime.

The second essential of popular participation in government is that the terms of office of those who are chosen to rule should be so limited that changes of national judgment, arising from experience, from education, or from changed circumstances, may be made effective without rebellion or revolution.

The third essential is that the functions and powers of the ruling classes thus chosen should be restricted to those which are actually conferred in the choice. For this reason there can be no real and permanent democracy without a constitution. True democrats are jealous and zealous for the sanctity of the constitution. They know that it is the sea-wall between them and autocracy.

Now, where these three essentials exist,—a representative and equal suffrage, periodical opportunity for the people to change their rulers peacefully, and a careful limitation of official powers by the constitution,—there is genuine democracy.

Foreign critics say that the United States is not a truly democratic country, because the people are not all on a level, all alike. But when did democracy offer to guarantee the similarity of people, or grade mankind down to a dead flat? When all the trees in the forest have the same number of leaves, when all the rivers that flow into the sea contain the same number of fish, when all the fields in the farm bear the same crop, then will all men be alike in their power and skill, and consequently on a level in degree and station. Democracy is no miracle-worker, no infidel toward natural law. Democracy declares that men, unequal in their endowments, shall be equal in their rights to develop those endowments.

Classes must exist in every social order—ruling classes, teaching classes, agricultural classes, manufacturing classes, commercial classes. All these are in the labouring class, but their labour is divided. The moment you begin to divide labour you begin to differentiate men. The moment you have men developed, by different kinds of work, on different sides of their nature. you have classes.

What democracy says is that there shall be no fixed barriers between these classes. The ways and passages shall be open. Opportunity shall be free. Every talent shall have a chance to earn another talent. I think we may claim that this is the case in the United States, at least to a larger extent than ever before in the history of the world. Not all the farmers' boys in the country may become Presidents of the nation. That would be physically impossible. But any of them may do so, and several of them have done so. Some of them, like Henry Clay and Daniel Webster, attained such eminence and power that the Presidency could hardly have added to their fame.

These cases are not accidents. They are logical evidences of an equality among men in the only sense in which equality is possible—equality of opportunity. This equality is no nebulous dream of a state in which degree is abolished and every man is as mediocre as everybody else. It is a real escape from the tyranny of artificial and hereditary distinctions; a real approximation of position and fitness, honour and ability. It is safeguarded, and its effects are diffused in some measure through the whole fabric of social life, not by any mere legal enactment, but by something vastly stronger and more efficient: the state of mind which is created in the people by committing to them the choice of their own ruling classes. Herein is fulfilled the divine prophecy of democracy: "And their nobles shall be of themselves, and their governors shall proceed from the midst of them."

In regard to this democratic method of electing rulers there are some things which I should like to say, with as much emphasis and clearness as may be consistent with brevity.

It is the highest and most reasonable method.

In the case of ignorant, undeveloped peoples, with whom the impulse of resistance is stronger than the instinct of order, the other methods may be necessary for a time. But they are to be considered as educative, corrective, disciplinary. All peoples, like all children, should be regarded as on their way to self-rule. When they are able to maintain it, they are entitled to have it. All arguments against the democratic method, based on the weakness, folly, and selfishness of human nature, apply with greater force to the autocratic and automatic methods. The individual follies of a multitude of men often neutralise one another, leaving an active residuum of plain common sense. But for a fool king there is no natural antidote; and sometimes men have desperately found that the only way to set his head straight was to remove it.

It is said that democracies are peculiarly subject to the microbes of financial delusion and the resultant boom-fever and panic-chill. But the Mississippi Scheme and the South Sea Bubble flourished under monarchical institutions; and the worst-depreciated currencies in the world have been stamped with the image and superscription of kings or dictators.

It is said that democracies are reckless, extravagant, spendthrift, and that official dishonesty and corruption thrive in them. But it would be difficult to parallel the extravagance and corruption of the government of France under the Bourbons, in the history of any republic. The Russian railway across Siberia was built through a quagmire of public peculation as vast as the Empire itself.

It is said that democracies sometimes choose weak, incompetent, and even bad men for their ruling classes. So they do. But they have no monopoly in this respect. The automatic method of selecting rulers produced Charles II. and James II. and George III. It would be difficult to surpass in any republic the folly which selected Lord North to guide the policy of Great Britain at a time when Chatham, Fox, and Burke were on the stage. Yet this was done, not by an ignorant democracy, but by an automatic king. Nor does the autocratic plan of allowing rulers to choose themselves work any more infallibly. France had two examples of it in the last century. Napoleon I. was a catastrophe. Napoleon III. was a crime.

All that may be said of the propriety of appealing to Providence and trusting God for the ordaining of the powers that be, applies to the democratic method even more than to any other. ' Why should we suppose that Providence has anything more to do with the ambition of a strong man to climb a throne, than with the desire of a great people to make a strong man their leader? Why should we imagine that God is any more willing to direct the eugenics of royal marriages, and regulate the matrimonial alliances of titled personages, for the sake of producing proper kings and lords, than to guide the thoughts and desires of a great people and turn their hearts to the choice of good Presidents? The characteristic of democracy, says James Russell Lowell, is its habit of "asking the Powers that Be, at the most inconvenient moment, whether they are the Powers that Ought to Be." And what is this question but an appeal to the divine judgment and law?

There is as much room for Providence to act in the growth of public opinion as in the rise and propagation of a royal house. What royal house is there that goes so far to vindicate the ways of God to man as the succession of Presidents chosen by the people of the American Republic? Some of the choices have not been brilliant, a few have been unfortunate, not one has been evil or corrupt. There is no line of hereditary kings, no line of autocratic emperors, that claims as many great men, or half as many good men, in an equal period of time, as the line of Presidents of the United States.

There is warrant, then, in reason and in experience, for believing in the divine right of democracy. It is not the only righteous and lawful method of selecting rulers, but it is the highest and most reasonable. We lift our patriotism above the shallow and flashy enthusiasm for institutions merely because they are ours. We confide ourselves to the hopeful and progressive view of human nature, to the faith that God is able to make truth and right reason prevail in the arena of public opinion. We bless the memory of our first and greatest hero, because he had no desire for a crown, and so, by his personal influence, helped to make the choice of ruling classes in the United States neither autocratic nor automatic, but democratic.

But this method of providing for civil rule has its dangers, which cannot be denied, and which ought not to be forgotten.

Government by majority is not an infallible device for securing the best wisdom at any particular moment. It is a good working plan for conducting the experiments which need to be tried in order to determine, by success or failure, the direction in which the best wisdom lies. Our local failures ought to be as instructive as our general success. In our prosperity we should imitate the custom of the Romans, who sobered the joys of a public triumph by the presence of a monitor to warn the victor that he was not exempt from the dangers and frailties of mortality.

Three chief perils attend the democratic method of selecting the ruling classes:

The red peril of the rise of the demagogue.

The yellow peril of the dominance of wealth.

The black peril of the rule of the Boss.

There is a singular relationship among these perils. They are interwoven and concomitant. Unlike as are the men in whom they are separately embodied, the man through whom they all become possible is one and the same:—the celebrated "man with the hoe."

Hear a parable of the machine, the money-bag, the mouth, and the hoe. The man with the machine persuaded the man with the hoe to vote precisely according to orders, and thus made himself of much value as an agent of barter or an instrument of assessment. The man with the money-bag, desiring protection or power, went into the market-place and found there the man with the machine, whereupon these two discovered a community of interest.

48

This worked well until the man with the hoe grew suspicious that his part in the transaction, while the most important, was the least profitable. Then appeared the man with the mouth, promising to wind up the concern, distribute the assets, and alter the laws of nature so far as necessary to effect a universal exchange of hoes for money-bags. This programme was not fully carried out. But the machine was put temporarily out of repair; the money-bag was sent abroad for its health; the mouth had an opportunity to explain some of its promises and retract the rest; and the hoe, having marched in several processions and gained much experience, went back to hoeing as before.

I do not mean to say that this somewhat allegorical description has ever been completely realised, on any large scale in our country. But certain fragmentary features of it may be dimly recognised, here and there, in our politics. Men whose chief distinction is their wealth, men whose only profession is the manipulation of political wires, (underground,) men who are related to real statesmen as quacks to real physicians, have at times found their way into our ruling classes. Their presence is a menace to the integrity and security of the democracy.

Legislation hostile to wealth is political

brigandage. Legislation subservient to wealth is political suicide. It cannot be denied that "money talks." The thing to be prevented is that money should talk with more tongues than belong to it, and that it should say things that are neither true nor just, and that these things should be made laws for the people.

It is not likely that rich men, by virtue of their riches, will ever become the ruling class in this country, in the open. The natural operation of jealousy and envy will take care of that. The possession of a large estate, in the eyes of those who do not consider how it was acquired nor how it is used, will always be a cause of suspicion, often, as in the case of President Washington, most ungenerous and unjust. But that rich men should endeavour to control legislation, local and national, in their own interest, and to secure influence and thus to become a ruling class in secret, is more than likely. It is natural. It is a fact.

But what makes it possible in a democracy? No one could buy a vote if some one else were not willing to sell a vote. No one could run a legislature from his office if there were not a lobby at the capitol. No lobby could do business if there were not a machine. And no machine can fulfil the law of its own being without evolving a Boss. Here is the law of development of this species of political creature: First a party; then a faction; then a gang; then a clique; then a ring; then a Big Four, or Five, or Six; then a Boss.

There are States in this country where a single man has owned virtually all the offices, from the mayoralty of the biggest city down to the postmastership of the smallest village. There are cities in this country where the public franchises, the public pay-roll, and the public offices have been for years practically under the control of a secret society, and this secret society under control of a chief as autocratic as Rob Roy or Robin Hood. This is a ruling class with a vengeance. This is democracy deformed.

It would not be so bad, perhaps, if it were an intelligent, benevolent, public-spirited despotism. But, usually, this kind of rule is marked by shrewd ignorance, crass selfishness, bold dishonesty. Its dark consummate flower was William M. Tweed, of New York, who reigned over the city for seven years; stole $6,000,000 or more for himself, and $60,000,000 or more for his followers; was indorsed at the height of his corruption by six of the richest citizens of the metropolis; had a public statue offered to

him by *The New York Sun* as a "noble bene-
factor of the city"; and summed up his career,
at the time of his commitment to the peniten-
tiary, in the following conversation with the
warden:

"What is your occupation?" "Statesman."
"What is your religion?" "None."

It is an error to assume, and a crime to assert, that rulers of this type are common in
our country. The Tweeds are not normal;
they are exceptional. They have not yet become endemic, though in certain localities they
seem almost epidemic. They have not infected
the higher levels of national government, but
they have sometimes made themselves felt
there. And their presence, the power that
they wield through the poor man whom they
cajole and deceive, and through the rich man
whom they blackmail and serve, the possibilities of wider and deeper corruption which they
suggest, ought to remind us that the democratic method of selecting rulers, although, (or
perhaps because,) it is the highest and most
reasonable, needs to be all the more closely
watched, safeguarded, and defended against its
own inherent dangers.

What, then, is the safeguard of democracy
in the choice of the ruling classes? We have

certainly put all our eggs into the basket of popular suffrage. How shall we watch and protect that basket?

Education is the only possible safeguard which is in harmony with our principles and has the power to defend our institutions without enslaving them. I know not how this truth could be expressed more lucidly than it was stated in the charter of the University of Georgia in 1785:

"As it is the distinguishing happiness of her governments that civil order should be the result of choice and not of necessity, and the common wishes of the people become the law of the land, their public prosperity and even existence very much depend upon suitably forming the minds and morals of their citizens. . . . This is an influence beyond the reach of laws and punishments, and can be claimed only by religion and education."

"Platitudes!" some votary of novelty exclaims. Then so are virtue and honour and patriotism platitudes. It is by forgetting platitudes that men and nations are ruined. Platitudes are truths that are flat, level, and therefore fitted to use as foundations. It is by building on such foundations that social and political fabrics are made firm, square, and enduring.

IDEALS AND APPLICATIONS

"The first need of our country," said Lord Rosebery in his Rectorial Address before the University of Glasgow in 1900, "is the want of men. We want men for all sorts of high positions—first-rate men, if possible; if not, as nearly first-rate as may be."

But what means of producing first-rate men has been discovered, except education? I do not mean that kind of education which adorns a chosen few with the tinsel gewgaws of useless accomplishments. I mean that nobler education which aims to draw out and discipline all that is best in manhood—to make the mind clear and firm by study, the body strong and obedient by exercise, the moral sense confident and inflexible by disclosing the eternal principles upon which it rests.

What means except education can produce that other kind of men, whom Lord Rosebery did not mention, but who are no less essential to the welfare of a democracy—men who are capable of recognising first-rate men, and choosing them as rulers?

It is of little use for a republic to have higher institutions of learning producing men of wisdom and power, unless it has also a system of general, nay, of universal, education producing popular respect for humane wisdom and righteous power. The university at the summit, reaching as high as human intelligence can go, the common school at the base, spreading as wide as human nature itself, and between them the best attainable system of grammar schools and high schools and academies, and branching out from them an ever-developing organisation of technical and professional institutions—these are the defences of the republic.

It was the opinion of Thomas Jefferson that the best service he rendered to his countrymen was in the thought which he gave to the unfolding of this doctrine, and the work which he did to put it into practice in Virginia. Certainly there was no other way in which he showed more truly that he was a democrat.

Suppose, for example, that we are compelled to meet practically one of the dangers which are inherent in government by democracy. Suppose that by the extension of the suffrage the power of choosing rulers has come into the hands of a mass of comparatively ignorant voters like the negroes in some of the Southern States. They are coherent in action, because they are bound together by racial and social ties; incoherent in judgment, because their only real unity lies in the absence of knowledge and fixed principle. This coherent mass of incoherency, like a cargo of loose wheat in the hold of a ship, will imperil the equilibrium of the state in every hour of storm and stress.

The privilege of suffrage bestowed on ignorance is not a protection of natural rights; it is a detriment to them. It is like a diamond hung around the neck of a child, an invitation to kidnappers; like a can of dynamite in the hands of a fool, a prophecy of explosion. But how is the difficulty to be removed, the danger to be averted? Only two methods are possible: the restriction of the suffrage; the education of the ignorant.

The restriction of the suffrage is a temporary expedient. It may be wise, it may even be indispensable under certain conditions. Certainly there can be no objection to it, if it be accomplished through laws which are alike for all and uncoloured by prejudice. But at best it goes no further than that process which physicians call the encystment of a tumour. It shuts the evil up in a sac, but does not take it away. The man who does not know enough to be trusted with a vote can never be a pleasant or a safe neighbour. The man who is too ignorant to choose his own rulers will never be an easy citizen for any one to rule.

But education, though a slow remedy, is

thorough-going. It reaches the root of the disease. Wisdom and justice alike demand that the permanent cure should be used even while the temporary palliative is applied. A wise and loyal democracy will never restrict the suffrage by an educational qualification, without providing, at the same time, the educational privileges which will give all its citizens an opportunity to rise above the level of the restriction.

The amount of money to be expended by a democracy in public education is to be measured by the standard of intelligent manhood which it sets for its citizens. The standard, I say, for, after all, in these matters it is the silent ideal in the hearts of the people which moulds character and guides action. What is your ideal of a right American? The answer to that question will determine whether you think we ought to do more or less for popular education.

For my part, I reckon that, as the enlightenment and discipline of manhood are the best safeguards of a democracy, so they ought to be the objects of our chief care and our largest expenditure.

If our naval and military expenses surpass or even equal our educational expenses, we shall be on the wrong track. If we put the fortress and the fleet above, or even on a level with, the schoolhouse and the university, our sense of perspective will be out of focus. If we ever spend more to inspire awe and fear in other peoples than to cultivate intelligence and character in our own, we shall be on the road to the worst kind of bankruptcy,—a bankruptcy of men.

We want the common school more generously supported and more intelligently directed, so that the ability to read and think shall become the property of all, and so that the principles of morality, which must be based on religion, shall be taught to every American child. We want the door between the common school and the university wide open, so that the path which leads upward from the little red schoolhouse to the highest temple of learning shall be free, and the path that leads downward from academic halls to the lowliest dwelling and workshop of instruction shall be honourable. We want a community of interest and a co-operation of forces between the public-school teacher and the college faculty. We want academic freedom, so that the institutions of learning may be free from all suspicion of secret control by the money-bag or the machine. We want democratic universities, where a man is honoured only for what he is and what he knows. We want American education, so that every citizen shall not only believe in democracy, but know what it means, what it costs, and what it is worth.

III

THE PEOPLE RESPONSIBLE*

SAUL in Israel, Nebuchadnezzar in Babylon, Nero in Rome, William the Silent in Holland, Philip II. in Spain, George III. in Great Britain, Washington and Lincoln in America— all the powers that be, or have been, were ordained of God. And yet in every case the forces that have created them, and the causes that have exalted them, are to be sought in the character of the nations over which they have ruled. God ordains the power, but He ordains it to fit the people. A bandit-chief for a tribe of brigands, a tyrant for slaves, an inquisitor for bigots, a sovereign tax-collector for a nation of shop-keepers, a liberator for a race of freemen. The ruler is but the exponent of the inmost thoughts, desires, and ambitions of the ruled; sometimes their punishment, and sometimes their reward.

Therefore it may be said (subject to those

* Annual sermon before the Sons of the Revolution, February, 1895.

60

limitations and exceptions that are always understood among intelligent people when they speak in broad terms) that as a general law, the people are responsible for the character of their rulers.

There are some complications which obscure the operation of this law in a monarchy, an empire, or an oligarchy. A hereditary crown, a sword transformed into a sceptre, a transmitted title, gives an opportunity to usurp or extend unrighteous power.

But in a republic the truth emerges distinct and vivid, so that a child can read it. The rulers are chosen from the people by the people. The causes which produce the men, and raise them to office, and clothe them with authority, are in the heart of the people. Therefore in the long run, the people must be judged by, and answer for, the kind of men who rule over them.

When we test this law in the early history of the United States it gives us ground for gratitude. We have cause to "praise famous men and our fathers that begat us."

But shall our children and our children's children have the same cause to thank and esteem us? Shall they say of us, as we say of our fathers, "They were true patriots, who loved their country with a loyal, steadfast love, and desired it to be ruled by the best men"?

That depends on one thing. Not on the chance of war, the necessity of revolution, the coming of a national crisis. The obligation of patriotism is perennial and its occasion comes with every year. In peace or war, in prosperity or adversity, the true patriot is he who maintains the highest standard of honour, purity, and justice for his country's laws and rulers and actions. The true patriot is he who is as willing to sacrifice his time and strength and property to remove political shame and reform political corruption, as he would be ready to answer the call to battle against a foreign foe. The true patriot is he who works and votes, with the same courage that he would show in arms, in order that the aspirations of a noble people may be embodied in the noblest rulers. For, after all, when history completes the record and posterity pronounces the verdict, it is by the moral quality of their leaders and representatives that the patriotism of a people must be judged.

It is true that the sharp crisis of war flashes light upon this judgment. In the crisis of liberty, Washington stands foremost as the proof that the Revolution was for justice, not

for selfishness; for order, not for anarchy. In
the crisis of equality, Lincoln stands foremost
as the proof that the war for the Union was
not a war of conquest over the South, but a
war to deliver the captive and let the oppressed
go free. Those two men were the central figures
in the crises; but the causes which produced
them, and supported them in the focus of light,
while men of violence raged, and partisans
imagined a vain thing, were hidden in the
people's life and working in secret through
years of peace and preparation.

And when the third crisis comes—the crisis
of fraternity, in which it shall be determined
whether a vast people of all sorts and conditions
of men can live together in liberty and brotherhood, without standing armies or bloody re-
volts, without unjust laws which discriminate
between the rich and the poor, and crush the
vital force of individuality, and divide classes
—in liberty and fraternity, with the least possible restraint and the greatest possible security
of life and property and freedom of action—
when the imminent crisis comes in which this
hope of our forefathers must be destroyed or
fulfilled, the leaders who shall wreck or rescue
it will simply represent the moral character
and ideals of the American people.

IDEALS AND APPLICATIONS

The causes which control the development of national character are threefold: domestic, political, and religious: the home, the state, and the church.

The home comes first because it is the seed-plot and nursery of virtue. A noble nation of ignoble households is impossible. Our greatest peril to-day is in the decline of domestic morality, discipline, and piety. The degradation of the poor by overcrowding in great tenements, and the enervation of the rich by seclusion in luxurious palaces, threaten the purity and vigour of old-fashioned American · family life. If it vanishes, nothing can take its place. Show me a home where the tone of life is selfish, disorderly, or trivial, jaundiced by avarice, frivolized by fashion, or poisoned by moral scepticism; where success is worshiped and righteousness ignored; where there are two consciences, one for private and one for public use; where the boys are permitted to believe that religion has nothing to do with citizenship and that their object must be to get as much as possible from the state and to do as little as possible for it; where the girls are suffered to think that because they have no votes they have therefore no duties to the commonwealth, and that the crowning glory of an American woman's life is to marry a foreigner with a title—show me such a home, and I will show you a breeding-place of enemies of the Republic.

To the hands of women the ordinance of nature has committed the trust of training men for their country's service. A great general like Napoleon may be produced in a military school. A great diplomatist like Metternich may be developed in a court. A great philosopher like Hegel may be evolved in a university. But a great man like Washington can come only from a pure and noble home. The greatness, indeed, parental love cannot bestow; but the manliness is often a mother's gift. Teach your sons to respect themselves without asserting themselves. Teach them to think sound and wholesome thoughts, free from prejudice and passion. Teach them to speak the truth, even about their own party, and to pay their debts in the same money in which they were contracted, and to prefer poverty to dishonour. Teach them to worship God by doing some useful work, to live honestly and cheerfully in such a station as they are fit to fill, and to love their country with an unselfish and uplifting love. Then they may not all be Washingtons, but they will be

such men as will choose a Washington to be
their ruler and leader in

"The path of duty and the way to glory."

And in the conflict between corporate capital
and organised labour, if come it must, they
will stand fast as the soldiers, not of labour
nor of capital, but of that which is infinitely
above them both—the commonwealth of law
and order and freedom.

But the character of the people is not only
moulded by the tone of domestic and social
life, it is also expressed and influenced by the
tone of political life, by the ideals and standards
which prevail in the conduct of public affairs.
And here, it must be confessed, our country
discloses grave causes for anxiety. Our political
standards have undoubtedly shifted from that
foundation on which Washington placed them
in his first inaugural, "the principles of private
morality." Take, for example, the appearance
of governors of sovereign States who excuse
and defend the destruction of life and property
which would be called murder and arson if it
were the work of individuals, because it is committed by great labour-unions which control
public sentiment and votes. Take, for example,

66

the system of distributing public office as party spoils.

Without doubt, the Spoils System is an organised treason against the Republic and a transgression against the moral law. It is a gross and sordid iniquity. Its emblem should not be the eagle, but the pelican, because it has the largest pouch. It shamelessly defies three of the Ten Commandments. It lies, when it calls a public office part of "the spoils." It covets, when it desires to control that office for the benefit of party. It steals, when it converts that office from the service of the commonwealth into a gift to reward a partisan, or a sacrifice to placate a faction.

It is an idle amusement for clever cynics in the newspapers, and amiable citizens in their clubs, to vituperate the Ring and the Boss, while they approve, sanction, or even tolerate the vicious principle, "To the victors belong the spoils." This principle is the root of the evils which afflict us. There can be no real cure except one which is radical. Police investigations and periodical attempts to "drive the rascals out" do not go deep enough. We must see and say and feel that the whole spoils system from top to bottom is a flagrant immorality and a fertile mother of vices. The Ring does not form itself out of the air; it is bred in the system. A Boss is simply a boil, an evidence of bad blood in the body politic. Let the bad blood out and he will subside.

Who are responsible for the civic corruption of some of the American States and cities? The corporations from whom the Boss gets his wealth in payment for his protection; the office-seekers, high or low, who go to the Boss for a place for themselves or for others; and the citizens who, by voting or neglecting to vote, have year after year filled our legislative chambers with men who were willing to do the bidding of the Boss for a consideration. If there is to be a radical and permanent cleansing, it can only be by breaking up and eradicating the whole system of irresponsible and haphazard appointment to office, and by substituting for it the system of appointment for merit and fitness, under wise and just rules, which throw the civil service of nation, State, and city open, on equal terms, to every citizen who can prove that he is qualified to serve.

Think for a moment of what we have gained and what we have still to gain in this direction. There are 290,000 places in the Civil Service of the United States. Of these places, 154,000 have been classified under the rules. Since

1900, 59,000 have been added to the classified list. There are still 136,000 places which are outside of the classified service. It should be the desire and object of every patriotic American to remove these places as rapidly and as completely as possible from all chance of occupation or use by the spoils system. Burn the nests, and the rats will evacuate.

But what have religion and the church to do with all these things? Just this: a free church in a free state should exercise a direct influence upon the moral tone of domestic and political life. If not, it is an impotent and useless parody on Christianity. The church is set as a light in the world. Do not let that light be put into a dark lantern and turned backward upon the Scribes and Pharisees. Set it on a candlestick that it may give light unto all that are in the house. Let the church shed the light of warning and reproof upon the immoral citizen who enjoys the benefits of citizenship and evades its responsibilities; the dishonest merchant who uses part of his gains to purchase political protection and his good reputation to cover the transaction; the recreant preacher who denounces the corruptions of government "down in Judee" and ignores the same corruptions in the United States; the lawyers who study the laws in order to defend their clients in evading them; and the officials who profess to serve the state, and then add, "The state—that's *me.*"

But it is not only to expose and condemn the evil that the light of religion is needed. It should also shine to reveal and glorify the good. Let it fall upon the true heroes of the republic, the brave soldiers, the loyal citizens, the pure statesmen, that all men may know that the church recognises these men as servants of the most high God because they are in deed and in truth the servants of the people.

It is to be remembered that the American church bore a noble part in the beginning of our national life, inspiring, purifying, and blessing the struggle for justice and liberty. It is not to be forgotten that she has a duty, no less sacred, in the conflicts of these latter days; to encourage men in the maintenance of that liberty which has been achieved and in the reform of all evils which threaten the purity of private and public life; to proclaim that our prosperity does not depend upon the false maxims of what are called "practical politics," but, as Washington said, upon "religion and morality, those great pillars of human happiness, those firmest props of the duties of men, and citizens."

THE PEOPLE RESPONSIBLE

With politics, so far as they have to do with the strife of parties and the rivalry of candidates, the church has no concern. But with *polit-ethics*—the moral aspect of the life of the state —she must deal frankly and fearlessly. When she evades or neglects this office of public prophecy, when she gives her strength to theological subtlety and ecclesiastical rivalry and clerical millinery, and stands silent in the presence of corruption and indifferent to the progress of reform, her own bells will toll the death-knell of her influence; her sermons will be the funeral discourses of her power; and her music will be a processional to the grave of her lost honour. But when she proclaims to all people, without fear or favour, the necessity of a thorough-going conscience and a divine law of righteousness in every sphere of human life, the reverence of men will crown her walls with praise.

IV

THE AMERICANISM OF WASHINGTON
AND THE MEN WHO STOOD
WITH HIM *

HARD is the task of the man who at this late day attempts to say anything new about Washington. But perhaps it may be possible to unsay some of the things which have been said, and which, though they were once new, have never been strictly true.

Two of the things which need to be unsaid are these: first, that Washington was a solitary and inexplicable phenomenon of greatness; and second, that he was not truly an American, but an English country squire, transplanted.

Solitude, indeed, is the last quality that an intelligent student of his career would ascribe to him. Dignified and reserved he was, undoubtedly; and as this manner was natural to him, he won more true friends by using it than if he had disguised himself in a forced familiarity and worn his heart upon his sleeve. But

---

* An oration before the University of Pennsylvania, in the Philadelphia Academy of Music, February 22, 1906.

from first to last he was a man who did his work in the bonds of companionship, who trusted his comrades in the great enterprise even though they were not his intimates, and who neither sought nor occupied a lonely eminence of glory. He was not of the jealous race of those who

"Bear, like the Turk, no brother near the throne ;"

nor of the temper of George III, who chose his ministers for their vacuous compliancy. Washington was surrounded by men of similar though not of equal strength—Franklin, Hamilton, Knox, Greene, the Adamses, Jefferson, Madison. He stands in history not as a lonely volcanic peak like Mount Shasta, but as the central summit of a mountain range, with a fellowship of kindred peaks about him, enhancing his unquestioned supremacy by their glorious neighbourhood and their great support.

Among these men whose union in purpose and action made the strength and stability of the republic, Washington was first, not only in the largeness of his nature, the loftiness of his desires, and the vigour of his will, but also in that representative quality which fits a man to stand as the hero of a great people. He had an instinctive power to divine, amid the confusions of rival interests and the cries of factional strife, the new aims and hopes, the vital needs and aspirations, which were the common inspiration of the people's cause and the creative forces of the American nation. The power to understand these, the faith to believe in them, and the unselfish courage to live for them were the central factors of Washington's life, the heart and fountain of his serene Americanism.

It was denied during his lifetime, for a little while, by those who envied his greatness, resented his leadership, and sought to shake him from his lofty place. But he stood secure and imperturbable, while that denial, like many another blast of ill-scented wind, passed into nothingness, even before the disappearance of the party strife out of whose fermentation it had arisen. By the unanimous judgment of his countrymen for two generations after his death he was hailed as *Pater Patriæ*. The age which conferred that title was too ingenuous to suppose that the father could be of a different race from his own offspring.

But the modern doubt is more subtle, more curious, more refined in its methods. It does not spring, as the old denial did, from a partisan hatred, which would seek to discredit Washington by an accusation of undue partiality for

England, and thus to break his hold upon the people. It arises, rather, from a modern theory of what true Americanism really is: a theory which goes back, indeed, for its inspiration to Doctor Johnson's somewhat crudely expressed opinion that "the Americans were a race whom no other mortals could wish to resemble"; but which, in its later form, takes counsel with those British connoisseurs who demand of their typical American not depravity of morals but deprivation of manners, not vice of heart but vulgarity of speech, not badness but bumptiousness, and at least enough of eccentricity to make him amusing to cultivated people.

Not a few of our professors and critics are inclined to accept some features of this view, perhaps in mere reaction from the unamusing character of their own existence. They are not quite ready to subscribe to Mr. Kipling's statement that the real American is

"Unkempt, disreputable, vast,"

but they are willing to admit that it will not do for him to be prudent, orderly, dignified. He must have a touch of picturesque rudeness, a red shirt in his mental as well as his sartorial outfit. The poetry that expresses him must recognise no metrical rules. The art that de-

picts him must use the primitive colours and lay
them on thick.

Traces of this curious theory of Americanism
in its application to Washington may be found
in many places. You may hear historians describe him as a transplanted English commoner,
a second edition of John Hampden. You may
read, in a famous poem, of Lincoln as

"New birth of our new soil, the first American."

That Lincoln was one of the greatest Americans,
glorious in the largeness of his heart, the vigour
of his manhood, the heroism of his soul, none
can doubt. But to affirm that he was the first
American is to disown and disinherit Washington
and Franklin and Adams and Jefferson. Lincoln
himself would have rejected such an impoverish-
ing claim with huge and hearty laughter. He
knew that Grant and Sherman and Seward and
Farragut and the men who stood with him were
Americans, just as Washington knew that the
Boston maltster, and the Pennsylvania printer,
and the Rhode Island anchor-smith, and the New
Jersey preacher, and the New York lawyer, and
the men who stood with him were Americans.

He knew it, and by what divination? By a
test more true than any mere peculiarity of
manners, dress, or speech; by a touchstone able

to divide the gold of essential character from the alloy of superficial characteristics; by a standard which disregarded alike Franklin's fur cap and Putnam's old felt hat, Morgan's leather leggings and Witherspoon's black silk gown and John Adams's lace ruffles, to recognise and approve, beneath these various garbs, the vital sign of America woven into the souls of the men who belonged to her by a spiritual birthright.

What is true Americanism, and where does it reside? Not on the tongue, nor in the costume, nor among the transient social forms, refined or rude, which mottle the surface of human life. The log cabin has no monopoly of it, nor is it a fixture of the stately-pillared mansion. Its home is not on the frontier nor in the populous city, not among the trees of the forest nor the groves of Academe. Its dwelling is in the heart. It speaks a score of dialects but one language, follows a hundred paths to the same goal, performs a thousand kinds of service in loyalty to the same ideal which is its life.

True Americanism is this:

To believe that the inalienable rights of man to life, liberty, and the pursuit of happiness are given by God.

To believe that any form of power that tramples on these rights is unjust.

IDEALS AND APPLICATIONS

To believe that taxation without representation is tyranny, that government must rest upon the consent of the governed, and that the people should choose their own rulers.

To believe that freedom must be safeguarded by law and order, and that the end of freedom is fair play for all.

To believe not in a forced equality of conditions and estates, but in a true fairness of burdens, privileges, and opportunities.

To believe that union is as much a human necessity as liberty is a divine gift.

To believe, not that all people are good, but that the way to make them better is to trust the whole people.

To believe that a free state should offer an asylum to the oppressed, and an example of virtue, sobriety, and fair dealing to all nations.

To believe that for the existence and perpetuity of such a state a man should be willing to give his whole service, in property, in labour, and in life.

That is Americanism; an ideal embodying itself in action; a creed heated in the furnace of conviction and hammered into shape on the anvil of life; a vision commanding men to follow it. It was the subordination of the personal self to that ideal, that creed, that vision, which gave eminence and glory to Washington and the men who stood with him.

This is the truth that emerges, clear and luminous, from the conflicts and confusions of the Revolution. The men who were able to surrender themselves and all their interests to the loyal service of their ideal were the men who made good, the victors. The men who would not make that surrender, who sought selfish ends, who were controlled by personal ambition and the love of gain, who were willing to stoop to crooked means to advance their own fortunes, were the failures, the lost leaders, and, in some cases, the men whose names are preserved in their own infamy.

The ultimate secret of greatness is neither physical nor intellectual, but moral. It is the capacity to lose self in the service of something greater. It is the faith to see, the will to obey, and the strength to follow, an ideal.

Washington, no doubt, was pre-eminent among his contemporaries in natural endowments. Less brilliant in his mental gifts than some, less eloquent and accomplished than others, he had a rare balance of large powers which justified Lowell's phrase, "an imperial man." His bodily vigour and skill, his steadiness of nerve restraining an intensity of pas-

sion, his undaunted courage which refused no
necessary risks and his prudence which took
no unnecessary ones, the quiet sureness with
which he grasped large ideas and the pressing
energy with which he executed small tasks,
the breadth of his intelligence, the depth of
his convictions, his power to apply great
thoughts and principles to every-day affairs,
and his singular indifference to current prejudices and illusions—these were gifts in combination which would have made him distin-
guished in any company, in any age.

But what was it that won and kept a free
field for the exercise of these gifts? What was
it that secured for them a long, unbroken opportunity of development in the activities of
leadership, until they reached the summit of
their perfection? It was the evident magnanimity of the man. This assured the people
that he was no self-seeker who would betray
their interests for his own glory or rob them
for his own gain. This made the best spirits
of the time trust him implicitly, in war and
peace, as one who would never forget his simple duty in the sense of his own greatness.

From the first, Washington appears not as
a man aiming at prominence or power, but
rather as one under obligation to serve a cause.

THE AMERICANISM OF WASHINGTON

Necessity was laid upon him, and he met it willingly. After his marvellous escape from death in his first campaign for the defence of the colonies, in 1755, the Reverend Samuel Davies, fourth president of Princeton College, spoke of him in a sermon as "that heroic youth, Colonel Washington, whom I can but hope Providence has hitherto preserved in so signal a manner for some important service to his country." It was a prophetic voice, and Washington was not disobedient to the message. Chosen to command the Army of the Revolution in 1775, he confessed to his wife his deep reluctance to surrender the joys of home, acknowledged publicly his feeling that he was not equal to the great trust committed to him; and then, accepting it as thrown upon him "by a kind of destiny," he gave himself body and soul to its fulfilment, refusing all pay beyond the mere discharge of his expenses, and asking no other reward than the success of the cause which he served.

"Ah, but he was a rich man," cries the carping critic; "he could afford to do it." How many rich men to-day avail themselves of the opportunity to indulge in this kind of extravagance, toiling tremendously without a salary, neglecting their own estate for the public benefit, seeing their property diminished without complaint, and coming into serious financial embarrassment, even within sight of bankruptcy, as Washington did, merely for the gratification of a desire to serve the people? This is indeed a very singular and noble form of luxury. But the wealth which makes it possible neither accounts for its existence nor detracts from its glory. It is the fruit of a manhood superior alike to riches and to poverty, willing to risk all, and to use all, for the common good.

Was it in any sense a misfortune for the people of America, even the poorest among them, that there was a man able to advance sixty-four thousand dollars out of his own purse, (with no other security but his faith in their cause,) to pay his daily expenses while he was leading their armies? This unsecured loan was one of the very things, I doubt not, that helped to inspire general confidence. Even so the prophet Jeremiah purchased a field in Anathoth, in the days when Judah was captive to Babylon, paying down the money, seventeen shekels of silver, as a token of his faith that the land would some day be delivered from the enemy and restored to peaceful habitation.

THE AMERICANISM OF WASHINGTON

Washington's substantial pledge of property to the cause of liberty was repaid by a grateful country at the close of the war. But not a dollar of payment for the tremendous toil of body and mind, not a dollar for work "overtime," for indirect damages to his estate, for commissions on the benefits which he secured for the general enterprise, for the use of his name or the value of his counsel, would he receive.

A few years later, when his large sagacity perceived that the development of internal commerce was one of the first needs of the new country, at a time when he held no public office, he became president of a company for the extension of navigation on the rivers James and Potomac. The Legislature of Virginia proposed to give him a hundred and fifty shares of the stock. Washington refused this, or any other kind of pay, saying that he could serve the people better in the enterprise if he were known to have no selfish interest in it. He was not the kind of a man to reconcile himself to a gratuity, (which is the Latinised word for a "tip" offered to a person not in livery). If the modern methods of "coming in on the ground-floor" and "taking a rake-off" had been explained and suggested to him, I suspect that he would have described them in language more notable for its force than for its elegance.

It is true, of course, that the fortune which he so willingly imperilled and impaired, recouped itself again after peace was established; his industry and wisdom made him once more a rich man for those days. But what injustice was there in that? It is both natural and right that men who have risked their all to secure for the country at large what they could have secured for themselves by other means, should share in the general prosperity attendant upon the success of their efforts and sacrifices for the common good.

I am sick of the shallow judgment that ranks the worth of a man by his poverty or by his wealth at death. Many a selfish speculator dies poor. Many an unselfish patriot dies rich. It is not the possession of the dollar that cankers the soul, it is the worship of it. The true test of a man is this: Has he laboured for his own interest, or for the general welfare? Has he earned his money fairly or unfairly? Does he use it greedily or generously? What does it mean to him, a personal advantage over his fellow-men, or a personal opportunity of serving them?

THE AMERICANISM OF WASHINGTON

There are a hundred other points in Washington's career in which the same magnanimity is revealed in conduct. I see it in the wisdom with which he, a son of the South, chose most of his generals from the North, that he might secure immediate efficiency and unity in the army. I see it in the generosity with which he praised the achievements of his associates, disregarding jealous rivalries, and ever willing to share the credit of victory as he was to bear the burden of defeat. I see it in the patience with which he suffered his fame to be imperilled for the moment by reverses and retreats, if only he might the more surely guard the frail hope of ultimate victory for his country. I see it in the quiet dignity with which he faced the Conway Cabal, not anxious to defend his own reputation and secure his own power, but nobly resolute to save the army from being crippled and the cause of liberty from being wrecked. I see it in the splendid self-forgetfulness which cleansed his mind of all temptation to take personal revenge upon those who had sought to injure him in that base intrigue. I read it in his letter of consolation and encouragement to poor Gates after the defeat at Camden. I hear the prolonged re-echoing music of it in his letter to General Knox in 1798, in regard to military appointments, declaring his wish to "avoid feuds with those who are embarked in the same general enterprise with myself."

The same spirit speaks in his circular address to the governors of the different States, urging them to "forget their local prejudices and policies; to make those mutual concessions which are requisite to the general prosperity, and in some instances to sacrifice their individual advantages to the interest of the community." It guides him unerringly through the critical period of American history which lies between the success of the Revolution and the establishment of the nation, enabling him to avoid the pitfalls of sectional and partisan strife, and to use his great influence with the people in leading them out of the confusion of a weak confederacy into the strength of an indissoluble union of sovereign States.

See how he once more sets aside his personal preferences for a quiet country life, and risks his already secure popularity, together with his reputation for consistency, by obeying the voice which calls him to be a candidate for the Presidency. See how he chooses for the cabinet and for the Supreme Court, not an exclusive group of personal friends, but men who can be trusted to serve the great cause of Union with fidelity,—Jefferson, Randolph, Hamilton, Knox, John Jay, Wilson, Cushing, Rutledge. See how patiently and indomitably he gives himself to the toil of office, deriving from his exalted station no gain "beyond the lustre which may be reflected from its connection with a power of promoting human felicity." See how he retires, at last, to the longed-for joys of private life, confessing that his career has not been without errors of judgment, beseeching the Almighty that they may bring no harm to his country, and asking no other reward for his labours than to partake, "in the midst of my fellow-citizens, the benign influence of good laws under a free government, *the ever favourite object of my heart.*"

Sweet and stately words, revealing, through their calm reserve, the inmost secret of a life that did not flare with transient enthusiasm but glowed with unquenchable devotion to a cause! "The ever favourite object of my heart"—how quietly, how simply he discloses the source and origin of a sublime consecration, a lifelong heroism! Thus speaks the victor in calm retrospect of the long battle. But if you would know the intensity of the fire that burned within his breast you must go back to the dark and icy days of Valley Forge, and hear him cry in passion unrestrained: "If I know my own mind, I could offer myself a living sacrifice to the butchering enemy, provided that would contribute to the people's ease. I would be a living offering to the savage fury and die by inches to save the people."

"The ever favourite object of my heart!" I strike this note again and again, insisting upon it, harping upon it; for it is the key-note. It is the capacity to find such an object in the success of the people's cause, to follow it unselfishly, to serve it loyally, that distinguishes the men who stood with Washington and who deserve to share his fame.

Read the annals of the Revolution, and you will find everywhere this secret and searching test dividing the strong from the weak, the noble from the base, the heirs of glory from the inheritors of shame. It was the unwillingness to sink and forget self in the service of something greater that made the failures and wrecks of those tempestuous times, through which the single-hearted and the devoted pressed on to victory and honour.

Turn back to the battle of Saratoga. There were two Americans on that field who suffered under a great personal disappointment: Philip

Schuyler, who was unjustly supplanted in command of the army by General Gates; and Benedict Arnold, who was deprived by envy of his due share in the glory of winning the battle. Schuyler forgot his own injury in loyalty to the cause, offered to serve Gates in any capacity, and went straight on to the end of his life giving all that he had to his country. But in Arnold's heart the ever favourite object was not his country, but his own ambition; and the wound which his pride received at Saratoga rankled and festered and spread its poison through his whole nature, until at last he went forth from the camp, "a leper white as snow."

What was it that made Charles Lee, as fearless a man as ever lived, play the part of a coward in order to hide his treason at the battle of Monmouth? It was the inward-eating corruption of that selfish vanity which caused him to desire the defeat of an army whose command he had wished, but failed to attain. He had offered his sword to America for his own glory, and when that was denied him, he withdrew the offering, and died, as he had lived, to himself.

What was it that tarnished the fame of Gates and Wilkinson and Burr and Conway? What made their lives, and those of men like them, futile and inefficient compared with other men whose natural gifts were less? It was the taint of dominant selfishness that ran through their careers, now hiding itself, now breaking out in some act of malignity or treachery. Of the common interest they were reckless, provided they might advance their own. Disappointed in that ever favourite object of their hearts, they did not hesitate to imperil the cause in whose service they were enlisted.

Turn to other cases, in which a charitable judgment will impute no positive betrayal of trusts, but a defect of vision to recognise the claim of the higher ideal. Tory or Revolutionist a man might be, according to his temperament and conviction; but where a man begins with protests against tyranny and ends with subservience to it, we look for the cause. What was it that separated Joseph Galloway from Francis Hopkinson? It was Galloway's opinion that, while the struggle for independence might be justifiable, it could not be successful, and so he yielded to the temptation of a larger immediate reward under the British crown than could ever be given by the American Congress in which he had once served. What was it that divided the Reverend Jacob Duché from the Reverend John Witherspoon?

THE AMERICANISM OF WASHINGTON

It was Duché's fear that the cause for which he had prayed so eloquently in the first Continental Congress, was doomed after the capture of Philadelphia, and his unwillingness to go down with that cause instead of enjoying the comfortable fruits of his native wit and eloquence in an easy London chaplaincy. What was it that cut William Franklin off from his professedly prudent and worldly wise old father, Benjamin? It was the luxurious and benumbing charm of the royal governorship of New Jersey.

"Professedly prudent" is the phrase that I have chosen to apply to Benjamin Franklin. For the one thing that is clear, as we turn to look at him and the other men who stood with Washington, is that, whatever their philosophical professions may have been, they were not controlled by prudence. They were really imprudent, and at heart willing to take all risks of poverty and death in a struggle whose cause was just though its issue was dubious. If it be rashness to commit honour and life and property to a great adventure for the general good, then these men were rash to the verge of recklessness. They refused no peril, they withheld no sacrifice, in the following of their ideal.

I hear John Dickinson saying: "It is not

our duty to leave wealth to our children, but it is our duty to leave liberty to them. We have counted the cost of this contest, and we find nothing so dreadful as voluntary slavery." I see Samuel Adams, impoverished, living upon a pittance, hardly able to provide a decent coat for his back, rejecting with scorn the offered bribe of a profitable office, wealth, a title even, to win him from his allegiance to the cause of America. I see Robert Morris, the wealthy merchant, opening his purse and pledging his credit to support the Revolution, and later devoting all his fortune and his energy to restore and establish the financial honour of the Republic, with the memorable words, "The United States may command all that I have, except my integrity." I hear the proud John Adams saying to his wife, "I have accepted a seat in the House of Representatives, and thereby have consented to my own ruin, to your ruin, and the ruin of our children"; and I hear her reply, with the tears running down her face, "Well, I am willing in this cause to run all risks with you, and be ruined with you, if you are ruined." I see Benjamin Franklin, in the Congress of 1776, already past his seventieth year, prosperous, famous, by far the most celebrated man in America, accepting without

demur the difficult and dangerous mission to
France, and whispering to his friend, Doctor
Rush, "I am old and good for nothing, but as
the store-keepers say of their remnants of cloth,
'I am but a fag-end, and you may have me for
what you please.' "

Here is a man who will illustrate and prove,
perhaps better than any other of those who
stood with Washington, the point at which I
am aiming. There was no romance about old
Ben Franklin. He was shrewd, canny, humour-
ous. The chivalric Southerners disliked his
cool philosophy, and the solemn New-Eng-
landers mistrusted his warm jokes. He made
no extravagant claims for his own motives,
and some of his ways were not distinctly ideal.
He was full of prudential proverbs, and claimed
to be a follower of the theory of enlightened
self-interest. But there was not a faculty of
his wise old head which he did not put at the
service of his country, nor was there a pulse
of his slow and steady heart which did not beat
loyal to the cause of freedom.

He forfeited profitable office and sure pre-
ferment under the crown, for hard work, uncertain pay, and certain peril in behalf of the
colonies. He followed the inexorable logic,
step by step, which led him from the natural

93

rights of his countrymen to their liberty, from
their liberty to their independence. He endured with a grim humour the revilings of those
whom he called "malevolent critics and bug-
writers." He broke with his old and dear associates in England, writing to one of them,

"You and I were long friends; you are now
my enemy and I am Yours, B. FRANKLIN."

He never flinched or faltered at any sacrifice
of personal ease or interest to the demands of
his country. His patient, skilful, laborious
efforts in France did as much for the final victory of the American cause as any soldier's
sword. He yielded his own opinions in regard
to the method of making the treaty of peace
with England, and thereby imperilled for a
time his own prestige. He served as president
of Pennsylvania three times, devoting all his
salary to public benefactions. His influence
in the Constitutional Convention was steadfast on the side of union and harmony, though
in many things he differed from the prevailing
party. His voice was among those who hailed
Washington as the only possible candidate for
the Presidency. His last public act was a peti-
tion to Congress for the abolition of slavery.

THE AMERICANISM OF WASHINGTON

At his death the government had not yet settled his accounts in its service, and his country was left apparently his debtor; which, in a sense still larger and deeper, she must remain as long as liberty and union endure in the Republic.

Is not this, after all, the root of the whole matter? Is not this the thing that is vitally and essentially true of all those great men, clustering about Washington, whose fame we honour and revere with his? They all left the community, the commonwealth, the race, in debt to them. This was their purpose and the ever favourite object of their hearts. They were deliberate and joyful creditors. Renouncing the maxim of worldly wisdom which bids men "get all you can and keep all you get," they resolved rather to give all they had to advance the common cause, to use every benefit conferred upon them in the service of the general welfare, to bestow upon the world more than they received from it, and to leave a fair and unblotted account of business done with life which should show a clear balance in their favour.

Thus, in brief outline, and in words which seem poor and inadequate, I have ventured to interpret anew the story of Washington and

the men who stood with him: not as a stirring
ballad of battle and danger, in which the knights
ride valiantly, and are renowned for their
mighty strokes at the enemy in arms; not as
a philosophic epic, in which the development
of a great national idea is displayed, and the
struggle of opposing policies is traced to its
conclusion; but as a drama of the eternal conflict in the soul of man between self-interest
in its Protean forms, and loyalty to the right,
service to a cause, allegiance to an ideal.

Those great actors who played in it have
passed away, but the same drama still holds
the stage. The drop-curtain falls between the
acts; the scenery shifts; the music alters; but
the crisis and its issues are unchanged, and the
parts which you and I play are assigned to us
by our own choice of the ever favourite object of our hearts.

Men tell us that the age of ideals is past,
and that we are now come to the age of expediency, of polite indifference to moral standards, of careful attention to the bearing of
policies upon our own personal interests. Men
tell us that the rights of man are a poetic fiction, that democracy has nothing in it to command our allegiance unless it promotes our individual comfort and prosperity, and that the

whole duty of a citizen is to vote with his party and get an office for himself, or for some one who will look after him. Men tell us that to succeed means to get money, because with that all other good things can be secured. Men tell us that the one thing to do is to promote and protect the particular trade, or industry, or corporation in which we have a share: the laws of trade will work out that survival of the fittest which is the only real righteousness, and if we survive that will prove that we are fit. Men tell us that all beyond this is phantasy, dreaming, Sunday-school politics: there is nothing worth living for except to get on in the world; and nothing at all worth dying for, since the age of ideals is past.

It is past indeed for those who proclaim, or whisper, or in their hearts believe and in their lives obey, this black gospel. And what is to follow? An age of cruel and bitter jealousies between sections and classes; of hatred and strife between the Haves and the Have-nots; of futile contests between parties which have kept their names and confused their principles, so that no man can distinguish them except as the Ins and Outs. An age of greedy privilege and sullen poverty, of blatant luxury and curious envy, of rising palaces and vanishing

97

homes, of stupid frivolity and idiotic publico-mania; in which four hundred gilded fribbles give monkey-dinners and Louis Quinze revels, while four million ungilded gossips gape at them and read about them in the newspapers. An age when princes of finance buy protection from the representatives of a fierce democracy; when guardians of the savings which insure the lives of the poor, use them as a surplus to pay for the extravagances of the rich; and when men who have climbed above their fellows on golden ladders, tremble at the crack of the blackmailer's whip and come down at the call of an obscene newspaper. An age when the python of political corruption casts its rings about the neck of proud cities and sovereign States, and throttles honesty to silence and liberty to death. It is such an age, dark, con-fused, shameful, that the sceptic and the scorner must face, when they turn their backs upon those ancient shrines where the flames of faith and integrity and devotion are flickering like the deserted altar-fires of a forsaken worship.

But not for us who claim our heritage in blood and spirit from Washington and the men who stood with him,—not for us of other tribes and kindred who

"*Have found a fatherland upon this shore,*"

and learned the meaning of manhood beneath the shelter of liberty,—not for us, nor for our country, that dark apostasy, that dismal outlook! We see the palladium of the American ideal, goddess of the just eye, the unpolluted heart, the equal hand, standing as the image of Athene stood above the upper streams of Simois:

"It stood, and sun and moonshine rained their light
On the pure columns of its glen-built hall.
Backward and forward rolled the waves of fight
Round Troy—but while this stood Troy could not fall."

We see the heroes of the present conflict, the men whose allegiance is not to sections but to the whole people, the fearless champions of fair play. We hear from the chair of Washington a brave and honest voice which cries that our industrial problems must be solved not in the interest of capital, nor of labour, but of the whole people. We believe that the liberties which the heroes of old won with blood and sacrifice are ours to keep with labour and service.

"All that our fathers wrought
With true prophetic thought,
Must be defended."

99

IDEALS AND APPLICATIONS

No privilege that encroaches upon those liberties is to be endured. No lawless disorder that imperils them is to be sanctioned. No class that disregards or invades them is to be tolerated.

There is a life that is worth living now, as it was worth living in the former days, and that is the honest life, the useful life, cleansed by devotion to an ideal. There is a battle that is worth fighting now, as it was worth fighting then, and that is the battle for justice and equality.

To make our city and our State free in fact as well as in name; to break the rings that strangle real liberty, and to keep them broken; to cleanse, so far as in our power lies, the fountains of our national life from political, commercial, and social corruption; to teach our sons and daughters, by precept and example, the honour of serving such a country as America—that is work worthy of the finest manhood and womanhood. The well born are those who are born to do that work. The well bred are those who are bred to be proud of that work. The well educated are those who see deepest into the meaning and the necessity of that work. Nor shall their labour be for naught, nor the reward of their sacrifice fail them. For high

THE AMERICANISM OF WASHINGTON

in the firmament of human destiny are set the
stars of faith in mankind, and unselfish courage, and loyalty to the ideal. While they shine,
the Americanism of Washington and the men
who stood with him shall never die.

V

THE CHIVALRY OF LAFAYETTE *

IN the great Calendar of Freedom, September
6 is marked with a star to commemorate
the birth of a hero,—Gilbert Motier de la Fay-
ette.

He was one of Nature's noblemen, whose
hereditary rank of marquis was negligible compared with the loftiness of his character and
the honour of his achievement.

He was a legitimate Son of Liberty; dedicat-
ing his youth to her cause in a far land; spending his manhood in her service in his own country; and standing fast in his old age, undaunted
by defeat, wounds, imprisonment and poverty,
uncorrupted by the bribes and blandishments
of tyrants whether of the court or of the mob,
unconquerably loyal to his ideal of freedom
secured by law and democracy founded on
justice.

Rightly has his birthday been marked with

---

* An address delivered in the City Hall, New York, on the 160th An-
niversary of Lafayette's Birthday, September 6, 1917.

the hero-star. But to-day, in this year of grace and fiery trial, 1917, let us mark it with a double star. It stands for the indissoluble friendship of France and America—sealed a hundred and forty years ago with French blood in America —resealed and ratified now with American blood in France!

Yes, let us mark this day with a triple star. For now the forces, which the Hanoverian King George III and his fat-witted Tory ministry once arrayed against us on the field of Yorktown, stand with us in the fight for the world's liberation from the menace of autocracy. Long since has that battle which Lafayette and the French helped us to win borne the fruits of peace and victory. Long since has England realized that our resistance to her monarch was a defence of her own cause, and felt the truth of Tennyson's words,

> "What wonder if in noble heat
> These men thine arms withstood,
> Retaught the lesson thou hadst taught,
> And in thy spirit with thee fought!"

Long since has France escaped from the successive yokes of Bourbonism, Sans-culottism, and Bonapartism and fulfilled the deferred hope for which Lafayette laboured,—a free

IDEALS AND APPLICATIONS

government of a self-controlled people. Mark
this day with a triple star, for by the law of
spiritual affinity, stronger than any political alliance or dynastic conspiracy, a threefold con-
stellation has formed and risen in the international sky. Along the banks of the Yser and
the Somme, the Aisne and the Meuse, above
the heroes who give their lives to make the
world "safe for democracy," the sun of this
day sees floating side by side, the Tricolour,
the Union Jack, and the Stars-and-Stripes!

It would be superfluous for the speaker on
this occasion to describe, even in outline, the
well-known life of Lafayette which is set forth
in his *Memoirs* and in the biographies by Bay-
ard Tuckerman and Charlemagne Tower. It
would be presumptuous for him to try to add
to the glowing eulogies which have been pro-
nounced by such orators as Daniel Webster,
John Quincy Adams, Edward Everett, Caleb
Cushing, and only last year in this hall, by
John Finley, and by that beloved Ambassador
Jusserand who has done more than any man
since Lafayette to reveal and endear France
to America. Only one line is left open to me,
and that is to speak briefly of the personal quality of this man, which gave especial value to

the service which he rendered to our country and to his own,—a quality that shines with living splendour now on that fiery front which stretches from Ypres to Belfort, from the Trentino to the gateway of Trieste.

Nothing more eloquent has been said of Lafayette than the words in which Charles Fox, pleading for the aid of England to rescue him from an Austrian prison, described him to the British Parliament in 1796: "That noble character which will flourish in the annals of the world and live in the veneration of posterity when kings and the crowns they wear will be no more regarded than the dust to which they must return." But there is a clearer and deeper insight in what Sainte-Beuve wrote in 1838: "I believe that if Lafayette had lived in the Middle Ages, he would have been what he was in our own times, a *chevalier*, seeking still in his own way the triumph of the Rights of Man under the sign of the Holy Grail."

Of all that has been said about Lafayette I like these words best. They give the key-note of the character which we desire not only to praise, but also to understand. He was a true knight of liberty, a chevalier. The distinctive glory of his career lay not in military genius, though he had a touch of it; nor in political

sagacity, for he had none of it. The golden
secret of his inestimable service to America,
to France, to the world, lay in his whole-hearted
chivalry.

The first element of chivalry is enthusiasm—
a flame in the soul, a great love, a sovereign
passion.

From the moment when young Lafayette, a
junior officer in the French Musketeers, dining
with his commander in the garrison of Metz,
heard the Duke of Gloucester, a brother but
no great friend of George III, tell the story
of the fight for freedom in America, the heart
of the eighteen-year-old boy, to use his own
words, "enlisted"; the knight embraced his
lifelong quest.

I do not believe that he fully understood
it then as he did later when he wrote: "This
was the last struggle of Liberty; its defeat
would have left it without a refuge and without
a hope." No, in that first fine impulse of devotion there was less reasoning and more instinct. It was a *coup de foudre*,—love at first
sight. But it was real enough to carry him
through a hundred obstacles to the accomplishment of his fixed purpose of crossing the
ocean and offering his sword to America.

Everything was against him. The government of France, at peace with England, could not sanction the expedition of a French nobleman to join the rebels. He wisely forgot to ask for the sanction. His family and all his titled friends and relatives, (except his noble wife, a girl of seventeen,) opposed his plan as a crazy whim. He prudently stopped talking about it and quietly worked at it. The American Commissioner in Paris who had at first accepted his offer, and promised him the rank of major-general in the American forces, now discouraged him and said he could provide no ship for the voyage. He made the retort courteous by purchasing a ship at Bordeaux with his own money and offering a passage to twelve other French officers. The timid King, alarmed at the possible consequences of the action of this rash young man, forbade him to go, and issued one of those terrible *lettres de cachet* against him. · Lafayette was arrested and virtually made a prisoner. He escaped in disguise to a port in Spain, where his ship picked him up; and after a most sea-sickening voyage of fifty-four days, landed him on June 13, 1777, on the shore of a wild creek in South Carolina, where he groped his way at midnight to the door of a plantation. After the dogs had barked at him, he was received by the owner, Major

Huger, with all the warmth of Southern hospitality.

None of these experiences damped the enthusiasm of the young chevalier. He rejoiced in hardship. Everything pleased him. He wrote to his beloved wife, his "dear heart," in rapturous strain of the beauty of the land; the agreeable simplicity of the people among whom "all the citizens are brothers" and "the richest and the poorest are on the same social level," and above all of the charm of the American women who "are very beautiful, unaffected in manner, and of a charming neatness"!

Arriving in Philadelphia, after a slow and toilsome journey, he was rather coldly received by members of Congress, who were at that time surfeited with foreign officers of minor merit who demanded high command and pay. But Lafayette was of another type. He sent a frank and generous address to Congress in which he asked only two favours: "The one is, to serve without pay, at my own expense; the other is that I be allowed to serve at first as a volunteer." His offer was accepted, a commission as major-general was granted to him, and he was assigned, at his own request, to the staff of Washington, henceforth his adored chief.

THE CHIVALRY OF LAFAYETTE

Thus began one of the most perfect friendships in human annals,—the sublime Washington and the chivalrous Lafayette. Thus America enrolled in the cause of Liberty a most noble, perfect knight,—a man so brave that when he was wounded at Brandywine he fought on with the blood running out of his boots,—a man so devoted that he refused the command of an army to invade Canada because he detected in the offer a cabal against his chief,—a man so unselfish that at Monmouth he resigned the leadership of the troops to another without a murmur because his chief wished it,—a man so courteous that he neither took nor gave offense, but was always smoothing away jealousies and strifes between other officers,— a man so steadfast that he never relaxed his efforts until the alliance between France and America bore full fruit in the presence of the French fleet and the French army under Rochambeau at Yorktown,—and then, a man so high-minded that he would not advance to crush Cornwallis until Washington was present to command the final victory.

It was the youthful chivalry of this man that "so happily formed the first bond of union" between two great nations, to both of which his fame now belongs.

IDEALS AND APPLICATIONS

History repeats itself before our eyes. When the Potsdam war-lords struck their treacherous blow through Belgium at the breast of France, in August, 1914, the young heart of America "enlisted" in her cause,—the sacred cause of Liberty. In the air and in the ambulance, in the trenches and in the hospitals, thousands of the flower of our youth sprang to help France —volunteers, volunteers! They asked no official sanction; they disregarded and over-leaped all obstacles; they were mustered by enthusiasm and enrolled by devotion; they gave themselves as a true knight lays his gift at his lady's feet! Write the names of Victor Chapman, Richard Hall, Alan Seeger, and the many young heroes who followed them on the road to glorious death, in the roll of that order of chivalry which is headed by the name of Lafayette. Write also the names of those brave boys,—yes, and girls too,—whom danger spared, as it spared him, and who live on as he lived to serve the undying cause of freedom.

Let us not forget the peculiar and inestimable value of just such chivalry. It counts for more than numbers. It gives light and leading. Even as Lafayette's "*beau geste*" was a powerful influence in bringing France to our side in that first struggle, so the example of our heroic youth has been of great avail

THE CHIVALRY OF LAFAYETTE

among the potent, constant causes which have
brought America at last to her inevitable place
in this fight for democracy against tyranny.
The eloquent words in which President Wilson
announced the participation of our country
with France and Great Britain in this war, repeat and reverberate the very principles which
Lafayette voiced a hundred times, and in which
he lived and died.

Remember also, and especially at this hour,
the chivalrous tenacity with which he kept
his faith. He came to us at the darkest time
of our early history. The battle of Long Island
had put Washington's army to flight. The
ragged Continentals were freezing in their refuge at Valley Forge. The defenders seemed
unable to drive the invaders out, and the invaders unable to catch the defenders. It looked
like a drawn battle, a stalemate. Many declared the struggle vain, and cried out for a
conference, a compromise, a peace by arrangement. But Washington knew better than to
dishonour the sacrifice already made in order
to obtain a counterfeit of the thing he was fighting for. Lafayette stood with him. He had
enlisted not for a campaign, but for the war.
The word stalemate was not in his vocabulary.
The words that stood emblazoned there were
first, Victory; then, Liberty; then, Peace.

The chosen motto on his coat-of-arms was *cur non,—why not?* and the spirit of his life was to fight on.

Adsit omen! May his example be prophetic. In this time of trial the faint-hearted are once more talking of a drawn battle, and the fatuous friends of a false peace are calling for conference and compromise. Between truth and treachery there can be no conference, between democracy and autocracy no stalemate. There is but one thing to do: fight on till we reach a peace worth having. The President has just said that "the intolerable wrongs done in this war by the furious and brutal power of the Imperial German Government ought to be repaired." They shall be! He has pledged our country "to exert all its power and employ all its resources to bring the Government of the German Empire to terms and end this war." We shall be content with nothing less! When that is accomplished we shall rejoice with France and Britain in welcoming peace,—not a peace honourable to dishonour, but a peace worth having,—a peace that will be good for all mankind.

The task which you have laid upon me for this day has been but imperfectly fulfilled.

THE CHIVALRY OF LAFAYETTE

One word only remains to be spoken. Remember, I pray you, that the chivalry of Lafayette, —his enthusiasm, his devotion, his courage, his courtesy, his tenacity of noble purpose,— is the embodiment of the real spirit of France. Dismiss from your minds the silly Berlin talk about the French as a decadent race. Dismiss the superficial picture of a frivolous and fickle people which tourists have gathered in the parts of Paris prepared for their amusement. Dismiss even the mistaken reports of down-hearted friends who speak of a nation already "bled white" and ready to lie down and die. None of these things are true. I know the homes of France, and have warmed my heart at the fires of love and loyalty which glow there. I know the great schools and workshops of France and the steady industry which animates them. I know the battle-front of France.

I come from the world-famous fortress of Verdun,—its citadel, its ruined suburbs, its hospitals bombed by the barbarous Prussians, its far-flung trenches under fire. No drop of blood that falls there is white; it is all red. No man who fights there to defend his country dreams of surrender or understands the word stalemate. Serious, cheerful, fearless, indom-

113

itable, officers and soldiers, their thoughts are of victory, liberty, peace. The word with which they bade me farewell was the immortal phrase: "*On les aura*,"—"We shall get them!"

VI

HUMANE CULTURE OR GERMAN KULTUR *

EVERYBODY knows that there is a difference in meaning between the German word Kultur, and the word Culture as it is commonly used in English and French. The object of this paper is to trace a little more clearly the nature and effects of this difference.

The fact that the German word is spelled with a K and the English with a C is of no significance. It is one of those orthographical accidents which may occur even in the best regulated languages.

The fact that both words come from the same Latin root proves nothing in regard to their present connotation. In the wear and tear of usage, words from the same root often come to be not only different, but even positively opposed in their significance. Children of the same family may be not merely unlike but also actively hostile to each other, as in the celebrated case of Cain and Abel.

* A paper read before the American Academy of Arts and Letters, New York, March 13, 1919.

115

IDEALS AND APPLICATIONS

It seems to me that this is what happened to these two words. Springing from the same root they came to stand for two ideas so contrary that a conflict between them was almost inevitable. It was because of this contrariety that the Germans were not able to understand, much less to admire, the other peoples of the world. It was for the same reason that these other peoples, the English, the French, the Italians, the Americans, while admiring some German products, as for example potash-fertilisers, cutlery, Dresden china, and beer, found themselves unable to love Germany as a nation, and absolutely unwilling to submit to the imposition of her Kultur upon the world at the point of the sword in 1914.

This, in effect, is what Germany desired, resolved, and attempted to achieve, doubtless with a sincere pupose, and unquestionably by lawless means. You may read the sincerity of the purpose in the verses of the pious poet Emanuel Geibel:

> *"Und es mag am deutschen Wesen*
> *Einmal noch die Welt genesen."*

You may hear the threat to use lawless means in the words of the German Chancellor to the Reichstag:

CULTURE OR KULTUR

"The injustice we commit [in invading Belgium] we will try to make good as soon as our military aims have been attained. He who is menaced as we are . . . can only consider how to hack his way through (*durchhauen*)."

You may judge the enormity of the claim advanced by the words of General von der Goltz:

"The nineteenth century saw the German Empire: the twentieth century shall see a German world."

Now the existence of national leaders capable of entertaining and avowing such sentiments, and of a vast and prosperous people ready to accept and support their plans, and of an army of well-trained, obedient, and fanatical millions of simple soldiers eager to carry out their predatory designs upon the world, was due, in my opinion, to the essential intellectual and moral vice of German Kultur, which is diametrically opposed to the humane ideal of culture.

Doubtless there were many economic, political and geographical motives and causes in the great war of 1914. But from the point of view of a humble disciple of philosophy, art, and letters, I can see but one really important thing in it—the attempt of a narrow, racial, megalomaniac Kultur to impose itself upon mankind,

117

not by the persuasive influence of sweetness and light, but by the developed force of a national "will to power."

It was a separate and separating kind of civilization. As a system, clearly conceived and worked out, in school, university, community, industry, army, and court, it was wonderful. But the value of any system depends upon the ruling ideals which are at the heart of it. There were three false assumptions at the root of German Kultur which put it in antagonism to humane culture and made it a menace to mankind. First, the assumption that the Almighty made the German race superior to all other races of the world. Second, that God chose the House of Hohenzollern to rule the German race. Third, that under this predestination the German race had a right to do what it pleased to work out its claim to the domination of the world.

It would be absurd to say that all Germans ever accepted these three superstitions—these *Aberglauben*. But it would be senseless to ignore the fact that they have permeated and poisoned the extraordinary system of German Kultur.

Recall that luminous description of the aim and ideal of education which was given by

CULTURE OR KULTUR

Matthew Arnold in his simple, colloquial English way some forty years ago.

"Culture," said he, "means the acquainting ourselves with the best that has been known and said in the world, and thus with the history of the human spirit." That was a humane and liberal conception, at once conservative and progressive, recognising the unity of the human race, the value of universal standards, and the necessity of knowing what was best in the past in order to advance to something better in the future. It was based, obviously, not on outward authority, but upon the appeal of right reason to the individual.

German Kultur, on the contrary, was based on the authority of the state over the individual. It was a closely organised system of education and discipline, scholastic, social, political, and military, specifically designed to produce obstinate adherents and obedient servants for distinctively Teutonic ideals and ambitions.

I happened to be a student in Berlin, about 1878, when the so-called *Kulturkampf* was in progress. It was a struggle between Rome and Prussia for control of the educational system. I felt as the woman in the classic story did about the fight between her husband and the bear. Bismarck won.

119

IDEALS AND APPLICATIONS

It was at that time that one could see clearly the cleavage between Culture and Kultur.

The professors whom I most frequented, Dorner, and Weiss, and Hermann Grimm, belonged to the liberal Germany of the past. But the popular idol of the university at that moment was Heinrich von Treitschke. In order that you may understand the significance of this man and his followers in German Kultur, I give a few quotations from their writings.

"The German is a hero born, and believes that he can hack and hew his way through life." (H. v. Treitschke, "Politics," vol. I, p. 230.)

"The appeal to arms will be valid until the end of history, and therein lies the sacredness of war." (*Ib.*, p. 29.)

"No state can pledge its future to another. It knows no arbiter, and draws up all its treaties with this implied reservation. . . . Moreover, every sovereign State has the undoubted right to declare war at its pleasure, and is consequently entitled to repudiate its treaties." (*Ib.*, p. i, 28.)

His disciples and followers, Bernhardi, and a nameless crew of generals, university professors, high-school teachers, and preachers, went far beyond this.

Take a few words from General Bernhardi:

CULTURE OR KULTUR

"The proud conviction forces itself upon us with irresistible power that a high, if not the highest, importance for the entire development of the human race is ascribable to this German people." (General Bernhardi, *Germany and the Next War*, p. 72.)

"*World-power or downfall!* will be our rallying-cry." (*Ib.*, p. 154.)

"War is a biological necessity of the first importance, a regulative element in the life of mankind which cannot be dispensed with." (*Ib.*, p. 18.)

"Might is the supreme right, and the dispute as to what is right is decided by the arbitrament of war. War gives a biologically just decision." (*Ib.*, p. 23.)

Take a few more words from German preachers and instructors of the young.

"What does right matter to me? I have no need of it. What I can acquire by force, that I possess and enjoy; what I cannot obtain, I renounce, and I set up no pretensions to indefeasible right. . . . I have the right to do what I have the power to do." (M. Stirner, *Der Einzige und sein Eigentum*, p. 275.)

"Our belief is that the salvation of the whole Kultur of Europe depends upon the victory which German militarism is about to achieve."

IDEALS AND APPLICATIONS

(Manifesto signed by 3,500 *Hochschullehreren* [professors and lecturers], quoted by Professor U. v. Wilamowitz-Mollendorf, *Reden*, part II, p. 33.)

Take as a final specimen this extract from the *Weekly Paper for Young Germany*, January 25, 1913:

"When here on earth a battle is won by German arms and the faithful dead ascend to Heaven, a Potsdam lance-corporal will call the guard to the door, and 'old Fritz,' springing from his golden throne, will give the command to present arms. That is the Heaven of Young Germany !"

But it may be said that I am quoting private writers, personal teachers, to condemn the German education which led to the late abominable war and lost Germany the friendship of mankind. Well, then, let us quote a late imperial authority, the Count Wilhelm Hohenzollern himself.

He was a voluminous speaker, sometimes good, but always copious. In 1890 he assembled a so-called educational conference at Berlin. To this conference he said that "the School ought first of all to have opened the duel against Democracy." To this conference he declared: "Gentlemen, I am in need of soldiers—we ought to apply to the superior schools the organisation in force in our military and cadet schools."

The Emperor got what he wanted. He got a government system of education which blotted out the old German love of liberty and produced the new German adoration of autocracy. He got a system of education which impregnated the soul of his folk with the superstition of an almighty state, above morality, beyond responsibility, supreme over humanity—a state not founded on the people's will, but absolute in power over the people's life—a state not answerable to other states for its conduct nor to the conscience of mankind for its actions—a state whose sovereign law was its own necessity, whose great destiny was the empire of the world, and whose highest function was war. He got a system of education, wonderfully organised and co-ordinated, marvellously perfect in routine and detail, and completely designed to produce in the German mind as the result of science, philosophy, and literature misapplied, two monstrous false convictions, two fetich-faiths. First, that Germany is over all—*Deutschland über Alles ;* second, that the Kaiser is the All-Highest—*der Allerhöchste !*

Here are these fetich-faiths announced in his own words:

IDEALS AND APPLICATIONS

"Remember that the German people are chosen of God. On me—on me as the German Emperor, the spirit of God has descended. I am His weapon, His sword, and His vice-regent."

The effect of such a Kultur on literature and the other arts was lamentable. The architecture of modern Berlin, the sculpture of the Siegesallee, the alleged poetry of Hauptmann and Süderman are not things of beauty, but pains forever. The distance from Kant to Nietzsche measures a vast downward slope. Lessing and Goethe and Schiller have no posterity; they were all caught and devoured by the Ogre Kultur.

But while the effect of this system on letters and the fine arts was such as to leave the stage free for the display of the Kaiser's own talents, it also gave him what he said he most needed—soldiers, millions of them! Soldiers ready to sink their conscience in their obedience to the Almighty State and the All-Highest Kaiser. Soldiers ready under orders to violate all international pledges, all civilized rules of war, all restraints of humanity. Soldiers ready to invade neutral territory, to devastate and ruin peaceful lands, to burn villages, to poison wells, to attack hospitals and kill Red Cross nurses,

124

to shoot old men and women and priests, to sink merchant ships without warning and drown helpless passengers and crews, to butcher little children, to rape women, and to carry away girls into white slavery. Soldiers who answer to the words which the Kaiser spoke to his guard: "You have given yourselves to me body and soul. For you there is only one enemy, and that is my enemy. It may happen —I pray that God avert it—that I order you to shoot down your relations, your brothers, nay, your parents; but then without a murmur you must obey my commands."

We may see, then, without any academic obscurity, what German Kultur—a narrow, selfish, immoral organisation of education— means. It had an ingrowing mind, and a barbarous spirit. It has been beaten, absolutely, on its chosen field of battle. Now the question is, what shall be the fruit of victory?

Shall it be a relapse into the ancient chaos of international antagonisms based on mutual hatred and mistrust? Or shall it be an advance into a society of free nations pledged to maintain the pacific settlement of quarrels between nations on the basis of reason and justice?

We should hold fast to the ideal of Culture,

the knowledge and application of "the best that has been thought and said in the world." As we have approved the call to arms against barbaric Germanism, so we should approve the effort to establish a better understanding and a wiser co-operation among the nations. Americanitis should be as repugnant to us as Germanism. The power of our Republic should be dedicated to the good of the world.

Patriotism we believe in. Patriolatry we abjure and despise. We devote our efforts in art and letters not to any system of narrowing nationalist Kultur, but to the broad ideal of humane Culture, with its four aims of joy and power, sweetness and light.

The light of seeing things clearly and truly. The sweetness of imaginative vision by which we behold things old and new and enter into other hearts and lives. The joy of free and sane thinking for ourselves. The power of resolutely choosing, out of all knowledge and experience, the best to love, admire, and follow.

VII

HONOUR TO FRANCE *

IN our welcome to you, sir, as a brave soldier and a famous general, we would have you feel the warmth of America's friendship for France. That friendship we prize and treasure. Whatever happens in the whirligig of politics, America will not turn her back on France. We shall not count the war won, nor peace accomplished, until France is restored, whole and sound and safe against aggression or betrayal by her ancient foe.

Do not be disturbed, sir, by the confused and confusing noise of an American election. The Americans, like the French, are an excitable and talkative race. But underneath the talk are convictions and sentiments not easily changed. One of these is the sense of the debt of honour that we owe to France.

For the noble heart of Lafayette, who sprang to help us in our day of need, honour to France!

* Speech of welcome at the dinner to General Fayolle, representative of the French Government and army, given by the Lafayette Day National Committee, October 11, 1920, Waldorf-Astoria Hotel, New York.

IDEALS AND APPLICATIONS

For the long record of achievement in art and science and literature, honour to France!

For the steady faith that kept the idea of the Republic alive through fierce revolution, futile monarchy, and false empire, honour to France!

For the patience and industry with which she renewed her strength after the first German invasion, honour to France!

For the heroism with which she resisted the second German invasion and poured out her best blood in defence of freedom and right, and held the fort without flinching while she waited for her friends to come up, honour to France!

For the loyalty with which she consecrated the hour of victory to the cause of peace, and kept her word to enter the League of Nations against war, honour to France!

May our courage, our loyalty, our devotion, match hers! Our flag has floated close to hers on fields of bloody strife. May the Tricolour and the Stars and Stripes never be separated in the councils of world-wide peace.

ON RELIGION

VIII

CHRISTIANITY AND CURRENT LITERATURE

IN literature the inner life of man finds expression and lasting influence through written words. Races and nations have existed without it; but their life has been dumb and with their death their power has departed; they have vanished into thin air.

The Scythian, the Etruscan, the Phœnician are dead. The Greek, the Hebrew, the Roman still live. We know them. They are as real and potent as the Englishman, the American, the Frenchman. They touch us and move us through a vital literature.

Religion is a life—the life of the human spirit in contact with the divine. Therefore it needs a literature to express its meaning and perpetuate its power.

It is the fashion nowadays to speak scornfully of "a book religion." But where is the noble religion without a book? Men praise the "bookless Christ"; and the adjective serves as a left-handed criticism of his followers, who regard the Bible as their rule of faith and practice. True, he wrote no volume; but he absorbed one literature, the Old Testament; and he inspired another, the New Testament.

How wonderful, how supreme is the Bible as an utterance of life in literature! With what convincing candour are the hopes and fears, the joys and sorrows, the deep perplexities and clear visions of the heart of man under the divine process of education disclosed in its pages! What range! What history, biography, essays, epigrams, letters, poetry, fiction, drama—all are here. The thoughts breathe inspiration, the figures live and move. And most of all, the central figure, Jesus Christ, long expected, suddenly revealed, seen but for a brief time, imperishably remembered, trusted, and adored, stands out forever in the simple words of a few short chapters, the clearest, most enduring, most potent personality in the world's history.

I do not hold with the saying that "the Bible is the religion of Protestants." If that were true, Protestants would be in the position of mistaking the expression for the life, the lamp for the light, the stream for the fountain. But I hold that without the Bible, Christianity would lose its vital touch with the past, and much of its power upon the present. It would be like a plant torn from its roots and floating in the sea.

Christianity owes an immense part of its influence in the world to-day to the place of the Bible in current literature. What other volume is current in a sense so large and splendid? What book is so widely known, so often quoted, so deeply reverenced, so closely read by learned and simple, rich and poor, old and young? Wherever it comes it enriches and ennobles human life, opens common sources of consolation and cheer, helps men to understand and respect one another, gives a loftier tone to philosophy, a deeper meaning to history, and a purer light to poetry. Strange indeed is the theory of education that would exclude this book, which Huxley and Arnold called the most potent in the world for moral inspiration, from the modern school-house. Stranger still the theory of religion which would make of this book a manual of ecclesiastical propaganda rather than the master-volume of current literature.

"Beware of the man of one book," says the proverb. The saying has two meanings. The one-book man may be strong, and therefore masterful; he may also be narrow, and therefore dangerous. The Bible exercises its mightiest and most beneficent influence, not when it is substituted for all other books, but when it pervades literature.

Christianity needs not only a sacred Scripture for guidance, warning, instruction, inspiration, but also a continuous literature to express its life from age to age, to embody the ever-new experiences of religion in forms of beauty and power, to illuminate and interpret the problems of existence in the light of faith and hope and love.

Close this outlet of expression, cut off this avenue of communication, and you bring Christianity into a state of stagnation and congestion. Its processes of thought become hard, formal, mechanical; its feelings morbid, spasmodic, hysterical; its temper at once oversensitive and dictatorial. It grows suspicious of science, contemptuous of art, and alienated from all those broader human sympathies through which alone it can reach the outer world. Insulated, opinionated, petrified by self-complacency, it sits in a closed room, putting together the pieces of its puzzle-map of doctrine, and talking to itself in a theological dialect instead of speaking to the world in a universal language.

Books it may produce—books a-plenty! Big fat books of dogmatic exposition; little thin books of sentimental devotion; collections of sermons in innumerable volumes; pious puppet-show story-books in which the truth or falsehood of certain dogmas is illustrated by neatly labelled figures stuffed with sawdust and strung on wires. And these an insulated Christianity, scornful of what it calls mere literary art and unsanctified charm, would persuade us to accept as a proper religious library. But John Foster spoke the truth in his essay, *On Some of the Causes by which Evangelical Religion has been Rendered Unacceptable to Persons of Cultivated Taste*, when he calls these books "a vast exhibition of the most subordinate materials that can be called thought, in language too grovelling to be called style." Certainly they are not literature, nor is it to be wondered at or much regretted that they are not current. They do not propagate religion; they bury it.

Very different are the works by which the vital spirit of Christianity has been expressed, the vivifying influence of Christianity extended in the world of modern thought and feeling. There are sermons among them, like the discourses of South and Barrow and Liddon and Bushnell; and religious meditations like the *Confessions of St. Augustine* and *The Imitation of Christ;* and books of sacred reasoning like the *Provincial Letters* of Pascal, and Butler's *Anal-*

ogy of Natural and Revealed Religion; and divine
epics and lyrics like those of Dante and Milton
and George Herbert and Cowper and Keble.

But there are also books which are secular in
form, neither claiming nor recognizing ecclesiastical sanction, presenting life in its broad
human interest, and at the same time inevitably
revealing the ethical, the spiritual, the immortal
as the chief factors in the divine drama of man.

Christian literature includes the best of those
writings in which men have interpreted life and
nature from a Christian standpoint. The stand-
point does not need to be always defined or described. A man who looks from a mountain-
peak tells you not of the mountain on which he
stands, but of what he sees from it. It is not
necessary to name God in order to revere and
obey him. I find the same truth to life in *King
Lear* as in the drama of *Job :* and the same sublime, patient faith, though the one ends happily
and the other sadly. *The Book of Ruth* is no
more and no less Christian, to my mind, than
Tennyson's *Dora.* There is the same religion in
The Heart of Midlothian as in *The Book of Esther.*
Christ's parable of the rich man lives again in
Romola. In *Dr. Jekyll and Mr. Hyde* St. Paul's
text, "The flesh lusteth against the spirit," is
burned deep into the memory.

CHRISTIANITY AND LITERATURE

No great writer represents the whole of Christianity in its application to life. But I think that almost every great writer, since the religion of Jesus touched the leading races, has helped to reveal some new aspect of its beauty, to make clear some new secret of its sweet reasonableness, or to enforce some new lesson of its power. I read in Shakespeare the majesty of the moral law, in Victor Hugo the sacredness of childhood, in Goethe the glory of renunciation, in Wordsworth the joy of humility, in Tennyson the triumph of immortal love, in Browning the courage of faith, in Thackeray the ugliness of hypocrisy and the beauty of forgiveness, in George Eliot the supremacy of duty, in Dickens the divinity of kindness, and in Ruskin the dignity of service. Irving teaches me the lesson of simplehearted cheerfulness, Hawthorne shows me the intense reality of the inner life and the hatefulness of sin, Longfellow gives me the soft music of tranquil hope and earnest endeavour, Lowell makes me feel that we must give ourselves to our fellow men if we would bless them, and Whittier sings to me of human brotherhood and divine fatherhood. Are not these Christian lessons?

I do not ask my novelist to define and discuss his doctrinal position, or to tell me what religious denomination he belongs to. I ask him to tell me a story of life as it is, seen from the point of view of one who has caught from Christianity a conception of life as it ought to be.

I do not ask him to deal out poetic justice to all his characters, and shut the prison-doors on the bad people while he rings the wedding-bells for the good. I ask him only to show me good as good and evil as evil; to quicken my love for those who do their best, and deepen my scorn for those who do their worst; to give me a warmer sympathy with all sorts and conditions of men who are sincere and loyal and kind; to strengthen my faith that life is worth living even while he helps me to realize how hard it is to live; to leave me my optimism, but not to leave it stone-blind; not to depress me with cheap cynicism, nor to lull me with spurious sentimentalism, but to nourish and confirm my heart in Sir Walter Scott's manly faith, that "to every duty performed there is attached an inward satisfaction which deepens with the difficulty of the task and is its best reward."

The use of fiction either to defend or to attack some definite theological dogma seems to me illegitimate and absurd. I remember a devout and earnest brother who begged me to write a story to prove that Presbyterians never held the doctrine of infant damnation. I would as soon write a story to prove that Shakespeare was not the author of his own plays.

But that fiction may serve a noble purpose in renewing our attraction to virtue, in sharpening our abhorrence of selfishness and falsehood, in adding to the good report of the things that are pure and lovely, in showing that heroism is something better than "eccentricity tinged with vice," and in making us feel anew our own need of a divine forgiveness for our faults, and a divine Master to control our lives—that is true, beyond a doubt; for precisely that is what our best fiction from *Waverley* down to *The Bonnie Brier Bush* and *Sentimental Tommy* has been doing. Name half a dozen of the great English novels at random—*Henry Esmond, David Copperfield, The Cloister and the Hearth, Lorna Doone, Romola, The Scarlet Letter*—and who shall dare to deny that there is in these books an atmosphere which breathes of the vital truths and the best ideals of Christianity?

It must be admitted that there are many books, current at present, of which this cannot be said. Some of them breathe of patchouli and musk, some of stale beer and cigarettes, some of the gutter and the pest-house, many do not breathe at all. But I do not see in this any great or pressing danger. The chemists tell us that the paper on which these books are printed will not last twenty years. It will not need to last so long, for the vast majority of the books will be forgotten before their leaves disintegrate. Superficial, feeble, fatuous, inane, they pass into oblivion; and the literature which abides is that which recognises the moral conflict as the supreme interest of life, and the message of Christianity as the best promise of victory.

There are three mischievous and perilous tendencies in our modern world against which the spirit of Christianity, embodied in a sane and manly literature, can do much to guard us.

The first is the idolatry of military glory and conquest. It is one thing to admit that there are certain causes for which a Christian may lawfully take the sword; it is another thing to claim, as some do, that war in itself is better for a nation than peace, and to look chiefly to mighty armaments on land and sea as the instruments for the spread of civilization. The forerunner of Christ was not Samson, but John the Baptist. The kingdom of heaven cometh not with observation, nor with acquisition, nor with subjugation. If all the territory of the globe were subject to one conquering emperor to-day, no matter though the cross were blazoned on his banner and his throne, the kingdom of heaven would not be one whit nearer. "Not by might, nor by power, but by my spirit, saith the Lord." That is the message of Christianity. A literature that is Christian must exalt love, not only as the greatest, but as the strongest thing in the world. It must check and reprove the lust of conquest and the confidence of brute force. It must firmly vindicate and commend righteousness and fair-dealing and kindness, and the simple proclamation of the truth, as the means by which alone a better age can be brought nigh and all the tribes of earth taught to dwell together in peace. It must repeat Wordsworth's fine message:

> "*By the soul*
> *Only the nations shall be great and free.*"

The second perilous tendency is the idolatry of wealth. Money is condensed power. But it is condensed in a form which tends to canker and corrupt. A noble literature, truly in harmony with the spirit of Christ, will expose, with scorn and ridicule, the falsehood of the standard according to which the world, and too often the church, measure a man's worth by

141

his wealth. It will praise and honour simple manhood and womanhood. It will teach that true success is the triumph of character, and that true riches are of the heart.

The third perilous tendency is the spirit of frivolity. A British essayist in writing a life of Robert Browning lately took occasion to remark that the nineteenth century had already become incomprehensible because it took life so seriously. This was probably not intended as a compliment; but if the nineteenth century could hear the criticism it would have good reason to feel flattered. An age that does not take life seriously will get little out of it. One of the greatest services that Christianity can render to current literature is to inspire it with a nobler ambition and lift it to a higher level.

I remember a guide in the Adirondacks, "Old Mountain Phelps," who used to say that he liked to go to the top of a certain mountain as often as possible, because it gave him such a feeling of "heaven-up-histedness." That is an uncouth, eloquent phrase to describe the function of a great literature.

I want the books that help me out of the vacancy and despair of a frivolous mind, out of the tangle and confusion of a society that is

buried in *bric-à-brac,* out of the meanness of un-
feeling mockery and the heaviness of incessant
mirth, into a loftier and serener region. There,
through the clear air of serious thought, I can
learn to look soberly and bravely upon the
mingled misery and splendour of human existence, and then go down with a more cheerful
courage to play a man's part in the life which
Christ has forever ennobled by his divine presence.

IX

THE CHURCH IN THE CITY

THE very things that make the church most needed in the city are the things that make it hard for the church to survive there. The throng and pressure of life, the intensity of business competition and social emulation, the extravagance of wealth and the exigencies of poverty, the scarcity of time and the super-abundance of pastime, the presence of crowds and the absence of fellowship, the avarice-chill and the amusement-fever, the rush and whirl and glare and busy emptiness of a life at top speed—in these things the church finds its opportunity, its call, and its danger.

If the city church is to fill its place, and do its proper work, it must have two things: first, a clear idea of the mission to which Christ has appointed it; second, a firm purpose to fulfil that mission and not to die while there is work to do.

The church in the city is not to be conformed to the fashion of the surrounding world. It is a great mistake to suppose that men and women want from the city church what they can get, and do get, anywhere else in the city—glitter and bustle and display and rivalry and superficial entertainment. They want something very different; and that something is religion; and religion means inward purity and peace and joy, the sense of God's nearness, the comfort of Christ's love, the strength that comes from spiritual food and fellowship.

It may seem inconsistent to say this after what I have already said of the city. But truth generally resides in apparent contradictions. The characteristics of city life intensify the necessity of religion. The peril of the city church lies in the temptation to make itself an annex and an imitation, rather than a refuge and a contrast. The church must always be separate from the world, in the sense that the church has something distinct and different to offer. Not a Sunday lecture-hall, a sacred concert-room, an ecclesiastical millinery-shop, a baptised social club, or a disguised money-making corporation—none of these things does the city need from the church, but "a house of prayer for all nations"; a place where divine truth seems clearer, and human brotherhood more real, and heaven a little nearer, than anywhere else in the roaring town.

IDEALS AND APPLICATIONS

Separate from the world the church must be; but never shut off from the world. Not blind to the facts of city life, not insensible to its necessities, not indifferent to its peculiar and pressing problems, but wide-awake to all these things, close to the business and bosoms of the men and women for whose service it exists. The church must move forward with the tide of modern progress, keeping abreast of the development of the city in order that it may meet the city's need. The model described in the book of Genesis is a good model for a Noah's ark. But Noah has been dead for some time. The church is not an ark, but a life-boat. In building a life-boat you will do well to follow the most modern lines and use the latest equipment. The aim of the church is not to keep on doing the same thing forever in the same way, but to improve the way as often as may be necessary to keep on accomplishing the same thing.

The problem of denominationalism meets the city church. On this corner is a house of worship that is called Presbyterian, on the next one that is called Catholic, on the next one that is called Episcopalian, on the next one that is called Baptist or Methodist, and so on. What does this mean but that good people have different tastes and predilections in matters of form and formula? It does not mean that they are enemies. Let each church be true to its own type, and recognise that the city has room and need for all types. And if the types become less crude, less angular, less extreme, by virtue of friendly contact; if each learns something from the others, that also is natural and profitable. I should be ashamed if I could not worship gladly in any church where Christ is confessed; and I should be sorry if I had not some memories which make the church of my father and mother a little sweeter, a little more home-like, than any other. What the city demands of all the different kinds of churches is loyalty to type, liberty of growth, and largeness of heart and mind in common service.

The problem of institutionalism meets the city church. My personal conviction on that question can be put into a sentence. The church may well have a soup-kitchen, if it is needed; but the church ought never to be a soup-kitchen. That kind of beneficence which ministers to bodily need and has no word for the soul, that kind of social service which is carefully devitalised from all spiritual purpose, belongs, if anywhere, to the state, not to the church. When the church gives a cup of cold water to a little

147

child, it should be done in the Master's name.
When the church ministers to the sick, the
afflicted, the imprisoned, it should seek in them
what the Master sought—their souls, to save
them from sin. Bread? Yes, let the church
deal bread to the hungry, but never fail to give
a blessing with the bread.

The problem of success meets the city church.
Its work is costly, its situation is trying, it necessities are immediate. A city church will not
run long on the momentum of the past, nor
survive many years on the strength of a reputation. It must succeed or die. Yes, but what
does it mean for the church to succeed? Only
this: to win the affection, confidence, support,
and loyalty of the people, by doing its own work
and fulfilling its own mission. The church can
succeed only by deepening, strengthening, purifying, the influence of religion in the city. Success on any other basis—fashionable, financial,
sensational—means, for the church at least, a
living death.

True, you sometimes see a city church which
is distinctly separate from the world, rigidly
opposed to its fashions, very strict in discipline,
and very orthodox in doctrine, slowly shrivelling
up and dying out. Why? Because it has re-
frained from being conformed to the fashion

148

of the world? No! But because it has forgotten to be transformed by the renewing of
its mind. Because it has kept the righteousness
of the kingdom, and left out the peace and the
joy. Because its long prayers and strict rules
and correct doctrines have become dry, dull,
and mechanical. It has lost the note of spiritual gladness and power. It is losing its hold
on the city, not because it is too religious, but
because it is not quite religious enough to rejoice in God, and let its joy shine through. The
right kind of a church for the city is one which,
however simple its worship, however small its
congregation, is manifestly filled with the spirit
of consolation, love, and good cheer. Everyone who enters it feels at once, "These people
are glad to be Christians, and glad to have me
with them." Such a church will survive, and
in the best sense of the word succeed.

Somewhere I have read or heard a story of a
certain poor man who always used to go about
his work in such a spirit of joy and contentment,
with such beautiful visions shining in his eyes,
that he was called "the dreamer." When he
married, his home seemed to be full of the same
ideal peace and gladness. His wife and children
were visited by the same visions. When a
friend asked how it came to pass, the man con-

fessed that he carried around with him all the time the dream that he was a king, and that his wife was the queen, and that the boys and girls were princes and princesses. They all shared the dream, and they lived it out pleasantly together, so that every pleasure was a royal entertainment and every meal was a royal feast. Thus their common life was lifted up and beautified.

The dream of the poor man is the reality of religion. The message of the Gospel is that men and women are all sons and daughters of God. The church that brings this message and makes us feel its truth, amid the noise and turmoil and weariness and oppression of city life, is the right kind of a church for the city. It delivers us from bondage. It shows us how to be happy. It helps us to try to be good.

X

PROPERTY AND THEFT

THE relation of Christianity to communism
has become a question for religious people
to consider seriously, if they wish to preserve
their intellectual candour and self-respect. The
reason for this is curious and interesting.

The communists of the earlier type were for
the most part sturdy, and sometimes violent,
opponents of Christianity, and indeed of all reli-
gions, except such as they themselves occasionally invented. With this kind of communism,
men who sincerely professed to hold the Christian faith had, of course, no question of relation
to consider. It was already settled that it must
be war.

But in later times a new type of communism
arose, which laid aside the red cap and put on
the white cravat. It discussed the problem of
the organisation of society on ethical and religious grounds. "The real social unit," said the
teachers of this school, "is not the individual,
but the community, and a person is only a frac-
tion, who can have no right to possess anything

which the community needs or wants. The law which pretends to confer such a right upon an individual—the law which says, for example, that under certain conditions you may become the rightful owner of a piece of land, which you may use, or sell, or leave to your heirs, and which shall not be taken from you without due compensation—such a law is essentially immoral and irreligious, because it protects and rewards a form of selfishness. All things really belong to all men; and the man who wishes to gain a title to any portion of the earth, however small, is in effect willing to rob his fellow-men of that which God has given to them all in common. The idea of private property has something fundamentally unrighteous about it. The teachings of the Bible are against it. The spirit of Jesus, who was really a great socialist, is altogether in favour of common ownership. If those who profess to follow him were truly in sympathy with his doctrine and willing to apply it to every-day life, they would confess that what we now call property is only another form of theft, and would do their best, at all hazards, to abolish an institution so selfish, unjust, and unchristian."

Thus modern communism, at least in one of its manifestations, instead of professing hostility to Christianity, claimed alliance with it, and justified itself by an appeal to the moral and religious authority of the Bible. Not very long ago a candidate for the mayoralty of New York City (an honourable man, who polled sixty-seven thousand votes) affirmed that every man who owned his home was practically a robber of the community, and supported the accusation by quoting the Old Testament. A preacher, of wide fame and influence, declared from the pulpit that the early Christian church at Jerusalem was distinctly communistic, and that this is "the animus of the New Testament."

It is true that now the most modern prophets of communism have reverted to the old atheistic type. They have thrown off all pretense of seeking or desiring a divine sanction and authority for their proposals. They have taken an attitude of fierce hostility, or of scornful contempt toward religion. The manifesto of the Federation of Russian Workers in America says: "We hate religion. . . . We declare war upon all gods and religious fables. We are atheists." In Russia the Bolshevists began with a savage persecution of religion; but realising that this might defeat their own ends and add to the amount of fighting which they already had on their hands, they restrained the zeal of the more fanatical comrades, and at the Eighth Communist Congress, (March, 1919,) they formulated the Soviet policy of "organising the broadest possible scientific-educational and anti-religious propaganda." Bukharin, the editor of their principal newspaper, *Pravda*, says: "Between the precepts of communism and those of the Christian religion, there is an impassable barrier."

But in spite of this there still exists a considerable group of ingenuous and trustful persons, sincerely attached to the idea of religion, and desirous of adapting it to the most modern conditions, who insist that communism is in subliminal harmony with Christianity. They admit that the Bolshevists have their faults and have made mistakes. But they find in the apostles of the Soviet more to admire than to condemn. They regard Lenin and Trotzky as unconscious followers of the great Nazarene in many things. They hold that Bolshevism, despite its temporary errors, has uncovered the true path to a revival of the religion of the Bible by breaking down the unchristian institution of private property.

Assertions like these, when made by men of undoubted sincerity and benevolence, are not to be ignored. If Jesus really taught or believed that property is theft, then the church itself, like the temple of old, has become a den of thieves. If the animus of the New Testament is distinctly communistic, then every honest Christian is bound to obey its doctrine not only in the letter but in the spirit, and to work with those who are seeking to establish a new order of society in which private possessions shall be unknown.

No man can get any comfort or strength out of his religion if he even suspects himself of disloyalty to it in his daily transactions.

The sense of the terrible inequalities of human life under present conditions, the increased knowledge of the privations and sufferings of the poor, the misery that is condensed in great cities, the hardship that embitters toil in lonely and desolate regions, the dim consciousness of the manifold want and woe that men and women and little children are enduring in this tangled world, press heavily upon sensitive spirits in these days. If all this wretchedness were the fruit of a false social order, contrary to the law of God and the spirit of Christ; if the Bible revealed a remedy for it all in the doctrine of communism, which Christians were too ignorant or selfish or cowardly to accept or apply, then it would be no wonder that the people who play traitor to their own religion should find that it no longer brings them inward peace and joy.

They would deserve to be ill at ease, anxious, full of fears and forebodings. They would deserve to be of all men most miserable and fearful.

But suppose, after all, it should be true that human poverty and want and wretchedness do not spring from any single fault in the social order, but from a deeper source: the selfish and wilful evil that dwells in the heart of man. Suppose that the remedy which Christianity reveals should turn out to be something very different from communism: not the abolition of private property, but the use and control of it by the spirit of fair play and wise love. Then the church, still feeling the pressure of human misery upon her heart, and confessing her want of greater wisdom and larger love in seeking to lighten the burdens of men, could yet face her problem with courage and a steady mind. She need have no sense of fatal inconsistency in declining the alliance which communism claims. She could try to follow the spirit of Christ more faithfully, without surrendering her leadership to the men who demand a social revolution.

This is the situation, then, which the activities of communism force us to face. Those who are sincere in accepting Christianity as the true religion, and the Bible as its rule of faith and practice, must meet the question fairly and consider it seriously. Was Jesus a communist at heart? Are the laws which enable men to own their homes, and to save money for their children, an offence to him? Or are the communists who defy those laws and seek to overthrow them by violence, telling the truth when they say that they are against him, and against all religion? What does the Bible really teach about property and theft?

Two cases are quoted from the Bible to prove that it has at least a partial leaning toward the communistic theory.

The first is the Hebrew Year of Jubilee, which is used as an argument for the nationalization of land.

Now, when we study the Old Testament carefully we find that there is not a word of historic record to show that the Year of Jubilee ever went into practical operation; nor is there a single passage to indicate that this peculiar institution, given to a peculiar people under peculiar circumstances, was ever intended to be an example for all nations at all times. To claim that it was, would be as unreasonable as to argue that the Jewish method of slaughtering animals should be imposed on all butchers.

But waiving these objections, and looking at

the Year of Jubilee as a possible model for legislation in our times, we see that it was actually
an iron-clad law of entail, more rigid than England has ever known. It provided that the
land should always remain in the families among
whom it had been divided at the conquest of
Canaan. It could neither be alienated by an
individual, nor confiscated by the state. If a
man was forced to sell his land by stress of poverty, the utmost that he could dispose of was a
title to the usufruct for as much of the fifty
years as might remain before the next Jubilee.
At any time he might redeem it; and at the end
of the fixed period every man inevitably "re-
turned unto his possession."

Suppose a company of Slavic immigrants arriving in Judea under the operation of this law:
they could have bought city property, for that
was specially exempt from its provisions; they
could have rented farms from the native aris-
tocracy; but not one of those Slavs, nor one of
their children, nor one of their grandchildren,
could ever have acquired a share in one square
inch of the soil of the country. Any man who
admires this system is at liberty to say so; but
it is hardly probable that any one will try to
put it into practice, nor does it look much like
what we commonly understand by the nation-

alization of land, which is to make the earth as free as the air and the light to all men.

The second case which is quoted from the Bible in favour of communism is the example of the early church at Jerusalem. It is described in the second and fourth chapters of *The Book of Acts.* The characteristic feature of it is, that the believers in Christ "were together and had all things common; and sold their possessions and goods, and parted them to all, as every man had need."

But surely this does not imply a denial of the rights of private property. For if an individual could not really own anything, how could there be any buying or selling? If the fact of birth gives every one an equal claim upon all the good things of the world, how could these Christians, a mere handful in the city, defend their funds against the Jews and the heathen? What right had they to confine their benefactions, as they did, to their fellow-believers, instead of sharing all things with their brother men? It would be an unfortunate thing for the widows and orphans of our great cities if the modern churches should adopt the strict plan of the Jerusalem Christians. For, in point of fact, their experiment was simply the exercise of the right of every man to do as he chooses with his own; and they chose to live together and help each other. It was a fraternal stock company for mutual aid and protection. No man was bound to come into it unless he wished; but if he did come in, he was bound to act honestly.

Read what St. Peter said to that hypocrite, Ananias, about his land: "While it remained, was it not thine own? And after it was sold, was it not in thine own power?" It would be difficult to imagine a stronger statement of the rights of property under the most trying circumstances. Of course it is possible for any band of men who like the Jerusalem system to re-establish it to-day; but its result of pauperism in the primitive church was not particularly encouraging, nor would it bring us one step nearer to the communistic ideal of general ownership and distribution by the state.

There are some other cases which are not frequently quoted by modern communists, but which have a direct bearing upon the doctrine of the Bible in regard to the rights of private property. There is the case of Naboth and his vineyard.

Naboth was a landholder. He had inherited a field from his ancestors. It belonged to him, and therefore no one else had a right to build on it or to cultivate it. The vines which he had planted there were his own. He could eat the grapes, or make wine out of them, or give them to the village children. The "unearned increment" which had come to that field from the building of the royal palace in the neighbourhood was a part of Naboth's property. He could do with it as he liked—keep it, or rent it, or sell it.

Ahab was a king. He represented the state. He was the anointed of the Lord, and he wanted that vineyard. He had not the nerve to take it by violence, nor the cleverness to squeeze Naboth out with a tax. So he tried to buy it, and failing, took to his bed and turned his face to the wall. But Queen Jezebel was a woman of larger resources. She contrived a plan to get rid of Naboth; and then she invited her husband to go down and enjoy the confiscated property. And as he stood in the vineyard, trembling with uncertain pleasure, that man of iron, Elijah the prophet, found him, and cursed him in the name of the just God, promising that his race should perish in shame because of the evil that he had done.

It was not merely because Ahab had connived at the death of a man. Many a king of Israel had done worse without incurring a special revelation of divine wrath. But Ahab had violated a sacred right of property. He had trampled upon a principle of justice which made that poor man's vineyard his own, to have and to hold against all comers, whether they were greedy kings or envious beggars. There is not the slightest hint that Naboth was wronging anybody in owning that land; but there is the plainest teaching that in trying to take it away from him against his will the king was a thief; and for that, the prophet promised that he should die among the dogs, that he should perish as a landless vagabond.

It must be admitted that the Old Testament holds out scanty encouragement to the advocates of communism. But perhaps we shall find something in the New Testament to support the notion that private property is unjust and ought to be speedily abolished.

What shall we say then of Jason of Thessalonica, and Lydia of Philippi, and Titus Justus of Corinth, and Philip of Cæsarea, who all received the apostles into their own houses? Were these people engaged in perpetuating a cruel and oppressive distinction between the rich and the poor?

Turn to the gospels. There was a man in Bethany named Lazarus, who had a house in which he sheltered the Christ whom the community had rejected. There was a man named Zaccheus, who was rich and who entertained Jesus at his own house. Is there any suggestion that the Master disapproved of these property owners? There was a man named Joseph of Arimathea, who had a garden and a new sepulchre in which he made a quiet resting-place for the body of him whom the people had despised and crucified. Was he a selfish robber?

Christianity never would have found a foot-hold in the world, it never would have survived the storms of early persecution, had it not been sheltered in its infancy by the rights of private property, which are founded in justice, and therefore are respected by all lovers of righteousness, Christian or heathen. It is difficult to see how the religion of Jesus could have sanctioned these rights more emphatically than by using them for its own holy purposes.

But someone may say that this is only the lower side of Christianity; that there is a higher side which enforces charity and unselfish benevolence and universal brotherhood; and that in the development of these things the lower side is destined to disappear, and communism will become the order of society. Truly, it would be difficult to exaggerate the emphasis which is laid not only by Christ and his apostles, but also by the Old Testament writers, upon the duties of kindness and generosity and compassion for the needy. But these teachings are perfectly consistent with those other instructions of the Bible which enjoin diligence in business, and fidelity to contracts, and respect for the property of others.

The Bible teaches that God owns the world. He distributes to every man according to his own good pleasure, conformably to general laws. Under the operation of these laws a man may acquire such a title to certain things that for any other man, or community of men, to attempt to disposses him without compensation is robbery. Nor is there any difference in this respect between the property of the rich and the property of the poor. If it be fairly acquired by honest industry, lawful inheritance, or just exchange, the one is as sacred as the other. The savings-banks of New York State hold $1,250,000,000 of deposits. Most of this money has been laid up by people who work for wages. And if the bulk of this capital should go, as it probably will, into the purchase of homes for families, the law of God still declares that it must neither be stolen nor confiscated, nor even coveted, by private robber or public thief.

PROPERTY AND THEFT

There is a fundamental and absolute difference between the doctrine of the Bible and the doctrine of communism. The Bible tells me that I must deal my bread to the hungry; communism tells the hungry that he may take it for himself. The Bible teaches that it is a sin to covet; communism says that covetousness is the new virtue which is to regenerate society. Communism maintains that every man who is born has a right to live; but the Bible says that "if a man will not work neither shall he eat"; and without eating, life is difficult. Communism holds up equality of condition as the ideal of Christianity; but Christ never mentions it. He tells us that we shall have the poor always with us, and charges us never to forget, despise, or neglect them. Christianity requires two things from every man who believes in it: first, to acquire his property only by just and righteous means; and, second, to "look not only on his own things, but also on the things of others."

This condemns the reckless greed of the gold-worshippers, and the cruelty of conscienceless corporations, and the dishonesty of law-dodging sharpers; but it condemns equally the communistic theories which propose to sweep away or disregard the rights of private ownership. When the communist says that the public lands which are still held by the state ought to be retained, or distributed according to a new system, he is simply propounding an economic theory which may or may not be sound. But when he says that the real estate which has become private property ought to be practically confiscated without compensation, he is simply teaching us to call robbery by a longer name. It is not a question of expediency; it is a question of righteousness.

I have entire confidence in the sincere philanthropy and generous motives of many of the men who have been drawn into a partial approval of communistic doctrines. I have a profound sympathy with them in hatred of all tyranny and oppression, in hearty desire for the amelioration of society and the relief of all unnecessary suffering. Surely that is at least one of the objects of Christianity, to improve the present condition of humanity, to make the whole world not only better, but also happier. If there are any men and women who live in fat contentment with their own physical comfort, and shut their ears to the cry of the distressed, they are not true disciples of the compassionate Jesus, and the Bible promises that they shall have a heavy reckoning at the day of judgment.

166

PROPERTY AND THEFT

But it does not seem likely that the evils of society can be cured by moving along the line of communism. History warns us that every experiment in that direction has been a failure. Free corn filled Rome with hungry idlers. The communistic poor laws of 1815 made England howl with want and shame and crime. There is no reason to suppose that men in the mass are any more wise or kind or benevolent than they are as individuals. The idea of an all-absorbing, all-controlling, all-disbursing state is a Frankenstein monster. Even to coquet with it in theory is to increase the miseries of society.

It is in the interest of no separate class, but of all mankind, that we hold fast to the old-fashioned doctrine of the rights of property coupled with the duties of charity. The asylums and hospitals of New York City now draw the greater part of their support from the benevolence of between three and four thousand persons. What will become of those institutions if the springs which feed them are destroyed? Does anyone think that the Board of Aldermen, or the Labour Party, or the city at large would do the work better?

The advocates of communism, in their revision of the Bible, would give us an improved

version of the parable of the Good Samaritan.
They would tell us that when the proud Levite
and the selfish Priest had passed by the
wounded man, a kind communist came down
that way and began to whisper in the sufferer's
ear: "My friend, you have been much in error.
You were a thief yourself when you were amass-
ing your private wealth; and these gentlemen
who have just relieved you of it with needless
violence have only begun, in a hasty and un-
justifiable manner, what must soon be done,
in a large and calm way, for the benefit of the
whole community." Whereupon, we are to suppose, the man was much enlightened and com-
forted, and would have become a useful member
of society,—if he had lived.

But Christ said that it was a Samaritan, a
man of property, riding on his own beast and
carrying a little spare capital in his pocket,
who lifted up the wounded stranger, and gave
him oil and wine, and brought him into a place
of security, and paid for his support. And to
everyone who hears the parable Christ says:
"Go and do thou likewise." Here is the open
secret of the regeneration of society in the form
of a picture.

If we want it in the form of a philosophy,
we may get it from St. Paul in five words:

168

PROPERTY AND THEFT

"Let him that stole, steal no more"—that is *reformation;* "but rather let him labour"—that is *industry;* "working with his hands that which is good"—that is *honesty;* "that he may have"—that is *property;* "to give to him that needeth"—that is *charity.*

ON EDUCATION AND CONDUCT

XI

THE FLOOD OF BOOKS

"THE world is cumbered with books," complained the wise man, two thousand years ago. "There are books here in Jerusalem and in Thebes and in Babylon and in Nineveh; even in Tyre and Sidon among the Phœnicians, no doubt one would find books. Still men go on scribbling down their thoughts and observations, in spite of the fact that there is nothing new under the sun. Where are the readers to come from, I wonder? For much study is a weariness of the flesh, and of making many books there is no end."

But what would the writer that was king say if he were alive to-day, when the annual output of books in this country alone is more than five thousand, and when the printing-press multiplies these volumes into more than five million copies? Doubtless he would be much astonished, and perhaps even more displeased. But I conjecture that he would go on writing his own books, and that when they were done he would look for a publisher. For each age has its own thoughts and feelings; and each man who is born with the impulse of authorship thinks that he has something to say to his age; and even if it is nothing more than a criticism of other men for writing so much and so poorly, he wants to say it in his own language.

Thomas Carlyle, talking volubly on the virtues of silence, represents a *rôle* which is never left out in the drama of literature.

After all, is it not better that a hundred unnecessary books should be published than that one good and useful book should be lost? Nature's law of parsimony is arrived at by a process of expense. The needless volumes, like the infertile seeds, soon sink out of sight; and the books that have life in them are taken care of by the readers who are waiting somewhere to receive and cherish them.

Reading is a habit. Writing is a gift. Both may be cultivated. But I suppose there is this difference between them: the habit may be acquired by any who will; the gift can be developed only by those who have it in them to begin with. How to discover it and make the best of it, and use the writing gift so that it shall supply the real needs and promote the finest results of the reading habit,—that is the problem.

THE FLOOD OF BOOKS

I do not know of any ready-made solution. The only way to work it out is for the writers to write as well as they can, and for the publishers to publish the best that they can get, and for the great company of readers to bring a healthy appetite, a clean taste, and a good digestion to the feast that is prepared for them. If anyone partakes not wisely but too much, that is his own fault.

No doubt a good many people are drawn to writing by slight and foolish motives, and they do their work foolishly and slightly. Every human occupation has a certain proportion of superficial workers, to whom the work seems less important than the pay. But in the guild of letters there are also men and women of the better sort, to whom each year brings sincere delight in their work for its own sake.

Year by year scholars have been sifting and arranging the results of their studies in great libraries. Observers of men and manners have been travelling and taking notes in strange lands and in the foreign parts of their own country. Teachers of life and morals have been trying to give their lessons a convincing and commanding form. Critics have been seeking to express the secrets of good work in arts and letters. Students of nature have been bringing together the

records of their companionship with birds and
beasts and flowers. Story-tellers have been following their dream-people through all kinds of
adventures to joyful or sorrowful ends. And
poets have been weaving their most delicate fancies and their deepest thoughts into
verse.

In what different places, and under what
various conditions these men and women have
been working! Some of them in great cities, in
rooms filled with books; others in quiet country
places, in little "dens" of bare and simple aspect;
some among the tranquillizing influences of the
mountains; others where they could feel the inspiration of an outlook over the tossing, limit-
less plains of the ocean; a few, perhaps, in tents
among the trees, or in boats on the sea—though,
for my part, I find it difficult to understand
how anyone can actually write outdoors. The
attractions of nature are so close and so com-
pelling that it is impossible to resist them.
Outdoors for seeing and hearing, thinking and
feeling! Indoors for writing!

It is pleasant to reflect upon the great amelioration which has been made in the "worldly lot"
of writers, by the increase and wider distribution
of the pecuniary rewards of authorship. It is
not necessary to go back to the age of Grub

Street for comparison. There has been a change
even since the days when Lowell wrote, "I cannot come [to New York] without any money,
and leave my wife with 62½ cents, such being
the budget brought in by my secretary of the
treasury this week"; and when Hawthorne's
friends had to make up a purse and send it to
him anonymously, to relieve the penury caused
by the loss of his position in the Custom-House
at Salem. Nowadays, people who certainly do
not write better than Lowell and Hawthorne,
find life very much easier. They travel freely;
they live in a comfortable house—some of them
have two—with plenty of books and pictures.
The man who would begrudge this improvement
in the condition of literary workers must have
an uncomfortable disposition to live with. It
is no more than the world has done for the
doctors and the lawyers. Have not the profits
of book-making, on the material and commercial side, advanced even more rapidly? The
wages of printers and paper-makers and book-
binders are larger. The fortunes of successful
publishers are increased. Why should not the
author have some share in the general prosperity?

Besides, it should be remembered that while
there has been a certain enlargement in the pay

of literary workers, it has not yet resulted in opulence among men of letters as a class. The principal gain has been along the line of enlarged opportunities and better remuneration for magazine, newspaper, and editorial work. Setting these aside, the number of people who make a good living by writing books is still very small. I will not even attempt to guess how many there are; it might precipitate a long correspondence. But it is safe to say that there are not fivescore in America. What a slight burden is the support of a hundred authors among 105,-000,000 people! Your share in the burden is a little less than one-millionth part of an author. What is that compared with the pleasure that you get out of new books, even though you are one of those severe people who profess to read none but old ones?

When I hear that the brilliant writer of "The Mountain of Derision" has just built a mansion at Laxedo, or that the author of "The Turning Point" is driving a high-powered automobile through the White Mountains, it does not cause me a single pang of discontent. My contribution to that mansion, according to the present rate of royalty, was about forty cents, and to the support of the equipage I have given perhaps thirty cents. In each case I received good value for my money,—pleasant and, I trust, not unprofitable hours. This expense irks me far less than the extra two dollars a ton that I shall probably have to pay for coal this winter.

But I would not be understood as agreeing to the general proposition that the possession of automobiles and the like is necessary, or even favourable, to the production of good literature. Of course, if a man has extraordinary luck, he may find some competent person to take care of his luxuries for him, while he gives himself to the enjoyment of his work, and lives almost as comfortably as if he had never become rich. But, as a rule, it may be taken for granted that plain living is congenial to high thinking. A writer in one of the English periodicals a couple of years ago put forth the theory that the increase of pessimism among authors was due to the eating of too much and too rich food. Among other illustrations he said that Ibsen was inordinately given to the pleasures of the table. However that may be, it is certain that the literary life, at its best, is one that demands a clear and steady mind, a free spirit, and great concentration of effort. The cares of a splendid establishment and the distractions of a complicated social life are not likely, in the majority of cases, to make it easier to do the best work.

IDEALS AND APPLICATIONS

Most of the great books, I suppose, have been written in rather small rooms.

The spirit of happiness also seems to have a partiality for quiet and simple lodgings. "We have a little room in the third story (back)," wrote Lowell in 1845, just after his marriage, "with white curtains trimmed with evergreen, and are as happy as two mortals can be."

There is the highest authority for believing that a man's life, even though he be an author, consists not in the abundance of things that he possesses. Rather is its real value to be sought in the quality of the ideas and feelings that possess him, and in the effort to embody them in his work.

The work is the great thing. The delight of clear and steady thought, of free and vivid imagination, of pure and strong emotion; the fascination of searching for the right words, which sometimes come in shoals like herring, so that the net can hardly contain them, and at other times are more shy and fugacious than the wary trout which refuse to be lured from their hiding-places; the pleasure of putting the fit phrase in the proper place, of making a conception stand out plain and firm with no more and no less than is needed for its expression, of doing justice to an imaginary character so

180

that it shall have its own life and significance in the world of fiction, of working a plot or an argument clean through to its inevitable close: these inward and unpurchasable joys are the best wages of the men and women who write.

What more will they get? Well, unless history forgets to repeat itself, their additional wages, their personal dividends under the profit-sharing system, so to speak, will be various. Some will probably get more than they deserve, others less.

The next best thing to the joy of work is the winning of gentle readers and friends who find some good in your book, and are grateful for it, and think kindly of you for writing it.

The next best thing to that is the recognition, by people who know, that your work is well done, and of fine quality. That is called fame, or glory, and the writer who professes to care nothing for it is probably deceiving himself, or else his liver is out of order. Real reputation, even of a modest kind and of a brief duration, is a good thing. An author ought to be able to be happy without it, but happier with it.

The next best thing to that is a good return in money from the sale of a book. There is nothing dishonourable in writing for money.

IDEALS AND APPLICATIONS

Samuel Johnson, in the days of his poverty, wrote *Rasselas* to pay the expenses of his mother's funeral.

But to take, by choice, a commercial view of authorship, to write always with an eye on the market, to turn out copious and indifferent stuff because there is a ready sale for it, to be guided in production by the fashion of the day rather than by the impulse of the mind,—that is the sure way to lose the power of doing good work.

The best writing is done for its own sake. In the choice of a subject, in the manner of working it out, in the details of form and illustration, style, and diction, an author cannot be too jealous in guarding his own preference, ideal, inspiration,—call it what you will. Otherwise his book will lack the touch of personality, of independence, of distinction. It is here, perhaps, that a large part of the modern output of books fails to come up to the best standard.

But when a piece of work has been done, freely, sincerely, thoroughly,—done as well as the writer can do it,—then it is safe. The new methods of paper-making and printing and binding, the modern system of publishing and advertising, the admirable skill of the artists who are now engaged in designing illustrations and book-covers and types, certainly cannot hurt the quality of a book, and may do a good deal to help its sale. For this the honest author, having finished his work as nearly as possible to his own satisfaction, and disposed of it for the best price obtainable, should be duly grateful.

Amid the making of many books, good literature is still produced, as it was in the days of Thackeray and Dickens, Carlyle and Ruskin, Tennyson and Browning, Irving and Hawthorne and Lowell and Emerson, out of the hearts of men and women who write because they love it, and who do their work in their own way because they know that, for them, it is the best way.

XII

BOOKS, LITERATURE, AND THE
PEOPLE *

L ET us begin by trying to distinguish between
the people and the public.

The public is that small portion of the people
which is in the foreground at the moment. It
is the mirror of passing fashions, the court of temporary judgments, the gramophone of new tunes.

The people is a broader, deeper word. It
means that great and comparatively silent mass
of men and women on which the public floats,
as the foam floats on the wave. It means that
community of human thought and feeling which
lies behind the talk of the day.

There are many publics, for they change
and pass. But the people are one.

In the realm of letters, as elsewhere, I hold
to the principles of democracy. The people do
not exist for the sake of literature: to give the
author fame, the publisher wealth, and books
a market. On the contrary, literature should

* A discourse made before the National Institute of Arts and Letters
at its first meeting, New York, January 30, 1900.

exist for the sake of the people: to refresh the weary, to console the sad, to hearten the dull and downcast, to increase man's interest in the world, his joy of living, and his sympathy with all sorts and conditions of men.

It is to be desired, no doubt, that the relation of American literature to the people should be made closer, deeper, and more potent, that it may not only express, but really enrich the common life, and so promote the liberty of the individual from the slavery of the superficial, and wisely guide and forward the community in the pursuit of true happiness. But while we desire a further advance in this direction, it is well for us to remember that no advance is possible without a recognition of the ground already gained. Pessimism never gets anywhere. It is a poor wagon that sets out with creaking and groaning. Let us cheerfully acknowledge that the relations of literature to the people are probably better to-day than they have ever been before in the history of the world.

Freedom is a great gain. Open libraries are signs of progress.

Books are easier of access and possession, at the present time, than any other kind of food. They have become comparatively cheap, partly through the expiration of copyrights, and partly through the reduction in the cost of manufacture. I cannot think that the loss involved for certain classes in either of these processes is to be weighed for a moment against the resulting advantage to the people. The best books are the easiest to get, and, upon the whole, they have the widest circulation. Notably this is true of the most beautiful, powerful, and precious of all books, the Bible, which is still the most popular and the cheapest book in the world.

Another good thing in which we must rejoice is the liberation of books from various kinds of oppression. The *Index Librorum Prohibitorum* still exists, but it is no longer what it used to be. The real officers of the Inquisition in the modern world of letters are the librarians; and, taken all in all, they exercise their power with mildness and beneficence.

The influence of party politics on the fate of books is almost extinct. The days of literary partisanship, when the *Edinburgh Review* scalped the Tory writers, while the *Quarterly* flayed the Liberals, are past.

The alleged tyranny of modern magazine editors is a gentle moral suasion compared with the despotism of the so-called patrons of art and letters in earlier times. Let anyone who thinks that there is too much literary log-rolling in the

present day turn back to the fawning dedica-
tions of the Renaissance and the age of Queen
Anne, and he will understand how far authorship has risen out of creeping subserviency into
independence and self-respect.

Certainly the condition of the realm of letters
is better, its relation to the people is closer, and
its influence on the world is greater than ever
before.

But this does not mean that there are no evils
to be removed, no dangers to be averted, and
no further steps to be taken in advance.

Books are now sold in the dry-goods shops.
No one can fairly object to that. But is there
not some objection to dealing in books as if they
were dry-goods?

All that is necessary, at present, to sell an un-
limited quantity of a new book is to sell the
first hundred thousand, and notify the public.
The rest will go by curiosity and imitation. Is
there no danger in substituting popularity for
perfection as the test of merit?

More than five thousand books are published
every year in England, and nearly as many in
America. It would be a selfish man who could
find fault with an industry which gives employ-
ment and support to such a large number of his
fellow-men. But has there not come, with this

plethora of production, an anæmia of criticism? That once rare disease, the *cacoëthes scribendi*, seems to have become endemic.

The public must like it, else it would not be so. But have the people no interests which will be imperilled if the landmarks of literary taste are lost in the sea of publication, and the art of literature is forgotten in the business of book-making?

Everyone knows what books are. But what is literature? It is the ark on the flood. It is the light on the candlestick. It is the flower among the leaves; the consummation of the plant's vitality, the crown of its beauty, and the treasure-house of its seeds. It is hard to define, easy to describe.

Literature is made up of those writings which translate the inner meanings of nature and life, in language of distinction and charm, touched with the personality of the author, into artistic forms of permanent interest. The best literature, then, is that which has the deepest significance, the most lucid style, the most vivid individuality, and the most enduring form.

On the last point contemporary judgment is but guesswork, but on the three other points it should not be impossible to form, nor improper to express, a definite opinion.

BOOKS, LITERATURE, PEOPLE

The qualities which make a book salable may easily be those which prevent it from belonging to literature. A man may make a very good living from his writings without being in any sense a man of letters. He has a perfect right to choose between the enrichment of the world by working along the line of his own highest ideal, and the increase of his bank account by running along the trolley-car track of the public fancy. He has the right to choose, and his choice places him.

On the other hand, the fact that a book does not sell is not in itself a sufficient proof that it is great. Poor books, as well as good ones, have often been unsuccessful at the start. The difference is that the poor ones remain unsuccessful at the finish. The writer who says that he would feel disgraced by a sale of fifty thousand copies cheers himself with a wine pressed from sour grapes, and very unwholesome. There is no reason why a book which appeals only to the author should be considered better than a book which appeals only to the public.

Neither is there any reason why a publisher of popular books should go to the opposite extreme and say that "there is no use under heaven for the critic; the man who buys the book is the real critic, and so discriminating is he that a publisher cannot sell a bad book." If this standard prevails, we shall soon hear the proud and happy publisher saying of a book in its hundredth thousand, as Gregory the Great is reported to have said of the Scripture, that "he would blush to have it subjected to the rules of grammar."

The true cause for blushing lies in the fact that criticism has been so much confused with advertisement; that so many of the journals which should be the teachers of the public have become its courtiers; that realism in its desire to be dramatic has so often turned to the theatre instead of to real life, and thus has become melodramatic; that virility (which is a good word in its place) has been so much overworked, and used as a cloak to cover a multitude of sins; and that the distinction between books and literature has been so often overlooked and so largely forgotten.

The public is content with the standard of salability. The prigs are content with the standard of preciosity. The people need and deserve a better standard. It should be a point of honour with men of letters to maintain it by word and deed.

Literature has its permanent marks. It is a connected growth, and its life-history is unbroken. Masterpieces have never been produced by men who have had no masters. Reverence for good work is the foundation of literary character. The refusal to praise bad work, or to imitate it, is an author's personal chastity.

Good work is the most honourable and lasting thing in the world. Four elements enter into good work in literature:

An original impulse—either a new idea, or a new sense of the value of an idea.

A first-hand study of the subject and the material.

A patient, joyful, unsparing labour for the perfection of form.

A human aim—to cheer, console, purify, or ennoble life. Without this aim literature has never sent an arrow close to the mark.

It is only by good work that men of letters can justify their claim to a place in the world. The father of Thomas Carlyle was a stonemason, whose walls stood true and needed no rebuilding. Carlyle's prayer was: "Let me write my books as he built his houses."

XIII

CREATIVE EDUCATION *

IN that admirable book, *The American Com-monwealth*, by Mr. James Bryce, the chapter on colleges and universities comes immediately after the chapter on Wall Street. There is a singular contrast between them: for, while the one represents the nearest approach to pessimism in an uncommonly cheerful book, the other marks the highest note of optimism to which a British writer can allow his impressions to rise. The Wall Street chapter closes with the melancholy remark that the habits of speculation, constitutional excitability, and high nervous tension seem to have passed into the fibre of the American people. But the chapter on colleges and universities ends with the hopeful observation that, "while of all the institutions of the country they are those of which the Americans speak most modestly, and indeed deprecatingly, they are those which seem to be at this moment making the swiftest prog-

* Chancellor's Oration, Union University, Schenectady, New York, June 22, 1898. University of California, Charter Day Oration, in the Greek Theatre, March 23, 1905.

ress, and which have the brightest promise for the future."

In regard to the habit of modest and deprecating speech, we have a faint suspicion that the author's experience of academic anniversaries may have been limited. Perhaps he was here in the dull season. Perhaps he went only to Boston or Chicago.

But in regard to the recognition of our educational growth as one of the brightest and most promising features of the American commonwealth, there can be no doubt that it is an accurate observation and a wise judgment. No other expansion of the republic can be compared, in magnitude or in meaning, with the expansion of education. No other assurance of protection against those perils of American life which are popularly symbolized by Wall Street, can be compared with the fact that democratic communities have recognised the wisdom and the necessity of building up those safeguards of national sanity, integrity, and liberty which are typified, in their highest development, by the university.

It is to education that we look for protection against the spirit of

"Raw haste, half-sister to delay"—

193

against the blind and reckless temper of gambling—against the stupid idolatry of mere riches, either in the form of servile flattery or in the disguise of equally servile envy. Education must give us better standards of success and higher tests of greatness than gold can measure. Education must clarify public opinion, calm and allay popular excitability, tranquillize and steady American energy, dispel local and sectional prejudice, and strengthen the ties which bind together all parts of our common country.

Now, these are great expectations. We cannot hope to have them realised, even in part, unless we give to our whole educational effort, which is really bound together from the primary school up to the university, the highest aim, the true direction, the right movement. What, then, is the true ideal of education in a great democracy like the United States?

It is not a sufficient answer to this question to observe that since education is derived from the Latin *e-duco*, its true purpose must be the bringing out of what is in man. This definition is simple, but not satisfactory. There are many things in man, and there are various methods of bringing them out. The question is, What are the best things, and which is the best method of development?

CREATIVE EDUCATION

There is, for example, a method of bringing out the grain of wood by a combination of stain and varnish. It is a superficial way of enhancing the natural difference between pine and poplar and black walnut. Sometimes it is used as a device for disguising the difference between cherry and mahogany. Is this a true type of education?

There is also a method of bringing out the resources of the earth by working it for the largest immediate returns in the market. Farms are exhausted by overcropping; pastures desolated by overstocking; mines worked out for a record yield. Fictitious values are evolved and disposed of at transitory prices. Much that is marketable is brought out in this way. Is this a true type of education?

There is also a method of bringing out the possibilities of a living plant by culture, giving it the needed soil and nourishment, defending it from its natural enemies, strengthening its vitality and developing its best qualities. This method has been used, in recent experiments, in a way that seems almost miraculous, changing the bitter to the sweet, the useless to the useful, and proving that by a progressive regeneration one may hope in time to gather grapes of thorns and figs of thistles. Is this a true type of education?

IDEALS AND APPLICATIONS

These three illustrations of different methods of "bringing things out" represent in picture the three main educational ideals which men have followed. Back of our various academic schemes and theories, back of the propositions which are made by college presidents for the adoption of new methods or the revival of old methods, back of the fluent criticisms which are passed upon our common schools and universities, lies the question of the dominant aim in teaching and learning. What should be the ideal of education in a democracy—the decorative ideal, the marketable ideal, or the creative ideal?

I speak of the decorative ideal first, because, strangely enough, it is likely to take precedence in order of time, and certainly it is pre-eminent in worthlessness. Barbarous races prefer ornament to decency or comfort in dress. Alexander von Humboldt observed that the South American Indians would endure the greatest hardships in the matter of insufficient clothing rather than go without the luxury of brilliant paint to decorate their naked bodies. Herbert Spencer used this as an illustration of the preference of the ornamental to the useful in education.

The decorative conception of education seems

to be the acquisition of some knowledge or accomplishment which is singular. The impulse which produces it is not so much a craving for that which is really fine, as a repulsion from that which is supposed to be common. It is a desire to have something in the way of intellectual or social adornment which shall take the place of a mantle of peacock's feathers or a particularly rich and massive nosering.

This ideal not only rejects, contemns, and abhors the useful, but it exhibits its abhorrence by exalting, commending, and cherishing the useless, chiefly because it is less likely to be common. It lays the emphasis upon those things which have little or no relation to practical life. It speaks a language of its own which the people cannot understand. It pursues accomplishments whose chief virtue is that they are comparatively rare, and puts particular stress upon knowledge which is supposed to bestow a kind of gilding or enamel upon the mind. This ideal is apt to be especially potent in the beginning of a democracy, and to produce a crop of "young ladies' finishing schools" and "young gentlemen's polishing academies" singularly out of proportion to the real needs of the country. In its later development it brings forth all kinds of educational curiosities and abortions.

In this second crop of the decorative school of culture we find those strange phenomena of intellectual life which are known under the names of Æstheticism and Symbolism and Decadentism and the like. Their mark is eccentricity. Their aim is the visible separation of the cultured person from the common herd. His favourite poet must be one who is caviar to the vulgar. His chosen philosopher must be able to express himself with such obscurity that few, if any, can comprehend him. He must know more than anyone else about the things that are not worth knowing, and care very passionately for the things that are not usually considered worth caring about. He must believe that Homer and Dante and Milton and the Bible have been very much overrated, and carefully guard himself, as Oscar Wilde did in the presence of the ocean, from giving way to sentiments of vulgar admiration. His views of history must be based upon the principle of depreciating familiar heroes and whitewashing extraordinary villains. He must measure the worth of literature by its unpopularity, and find his chief joy in the consciousness that his tastes, his opinions, and his aspirations are unlike those of common people.

But the favourite sphere of decorative culture is the realm of art. For here it finds the way of distinction easiest and most open. The degradation and torpor, the spirit of ignorance and blind perversity which fell upon the arts of design and expression in the middle of the last century, and which still prevail to a considerable extent among those whom Matthew Arnold used to revile as the Philistines of England and America, made it necessary to begin a reform. Certain artists who were very much in earnest (call them pre-Raphaelites, or men of the new renaissance, or Impressionists, or musicians of the future, or what you will) took up the work, and won, together with a great deal of ridicule, a large reward of fame. In their wake has followed the motley throng of æsthetes, great and small, learned and unlearned, male and female and neuter; the people who talk about art because they think it is fine; who discover unutterable sentiments in beds and tables, stools and candlesticks; who go into raptures over a crook-necked Madonna after they have looked into their catalogues and discovered that it was painted by Botticelli; and who insist with ecstatic perversity that the worst of Wagner is better than the best of Beethoven. It is the veriest simian mimicry of artistic enthusiasm, a thing laughable to gods and men.

True art—large, generous, sincere—"the expression of noble emotions for right causes"— is a noble and ennobling study. But art as a fashion, with its cant, its affectation, its blind following of the blind, is a poor inanity. There is no use for it in a democracy—nor indeed anywhere in this world which was created by the Great Lover of Truth and Hater of Shams. The intellectual *poseur*, the shallow and self-satisfied æsthete is the last person who is entitled to set up a claim to the possession of the true theory and the ripe result of education.

At the opposite extreme from the decorative ideal lies the marketable ideal of education. Its object, broadly stated, is simply to bring out a man's natural abilities in such a way that he shall be able to get the largest return in money for his work in the practical affairs of life. Nothing is of value, according to this ideal, which is not of direct utility in a business or a profession. Nothing counts which has not an immediate cash value in the world's market.

CREATIVE EDUCATION

"Send my boy to high-school and college!" says the keen man of business. "What good will that do him? Seven years at the dead languages and higher mathematics will not teach him to make a sharp bargain or run a big enterprise." He thinks he has summed up the whole argument. But he has only begged the question. The very point at issue is whether the boy is a tool, to be ground and sharpened for practical use, or a living creature, whose highest value is to be realized by personal development.

The influence of this cash-value theory of culture may be seen in many directions.

It shows itself in certain features of our common-school system, not in the places where it is at its best, but in the places where it is controlled by politicians, sectarians, or cranks. It is far too mechanical. The children are run through a mill. They are crammed with rules and definitions, while their ideas and feelings are left to take care of themselves. Their imagination, that most potent factor of life, is intrusted to the guidance of the weekly story-paper, and their moral nature to the guidance of chance. The overworked and underpaid teacher is forced, by a false system of competition, to pack their little minds as full as possible of rules which they do not understand, and definitions which do not define, and assorted fragments of historical, geographical, chemical, mechanical, and physiological knowledge, which are supposed to have a probable market value.

It would be a good thing if the cities and towns of America would spend twice as much as they are spending to-day for common-school education. It would be a good thing if we could have twice as many teachers, and twice as intelligent, especially for the primary grades. And then it would be a good thing if we could sweep away half the "branches" that are now taught, and abolish two-thirds of the formal examinations, and make an end of competitions and prizes, and come down, or rather come up, to the plain work of teaching children to read intelligently and write clearly and cipher accurately—the foundation of a solid education.

The marketable ideal of culture makes itself felt, also, to a considerable extent, in some of the higher institutions of learning. We can trace its effects in the tendency to push the humanities aside, and to train the young idea, from the earliest possible period, upon the trellis of a particular trade. Every branch, every tendril which does not conform to these lines must be cut off. The importance of studies is to be measured by their direct effect upon professional and industrial success. The plan is to educate boys, not for living, but for making a living. They are to be cultivated not as men, but as journalists, surveyors, chemists, lawyers, physicians, manufacturers, mining engineers, sellers of wet and dry goods, bankers, accountants, and what not.

In obedience to this theory, the attention of the student is directed from the outset to those things for which he can see an immediate use in his chosen pursuit. Literature is spoken of in academic circles as a mere embellishment of the solid course; and philosophy is left to those odd fellows who are going into the ministry or into teaching. The library is no longer regarded as a spiritual palace where the student may live with the master-minds of all the ages. It has taken on the aspect of a dispensary where useful information can be procured in small doses for practical purposes. Half-endowed technical schools spring up all over the land, like mushrooms after a shower. We have institutes of everything, from stenography to farriery; it remains only to add a few more, such as an Academy of Mesmerism, a College of Mind Healing, and a Chiropodists' University, to round out the encyclopædia of complete culture according to the commercial ideal.

Let no one imagine that I mean to say a word against trade schools. On the contrary, I would speak most heartily in their support. So far as they do their work well they are an admirable and needful substitute for the earlier systems of apprenticeship for the various trades. Democracy needs them. They are really worth all the money that is put into them. But the error lies in supposing that they can take the place of the broader and higher education. By their own confession they move on another level. They mean business. But business is precisely the one thing which education does not mean. It may, doubtless it will, result in making a man able to do his own special work in a better spirit and with a finer skill. But this result is secondary, and not primary. It is accomplished by forgetting the specialty and exalting the man.

True education must begin and continue with a fine disregard of pecuniary returns. It must be catholic, genial, disinterested. Its object is to make the shoemaker go beyond his last—"*sutor ultra crepidam*"—and the clerk beyond his desk, and the surveyor beyond his chain, and the lawyer beyond his brief, and the doctor beyond his prescription, and the preacher beyond his sermon.

Special training, with an eye fixed on some practical pursuit, works directly the other way, and against the interests of a true democracy. It deepens the lines which separate men. It divides them into isolated trades which become close corporations, and into rival guilds which defend themselves by blocking all avenues of intercommunication.

But the right culture for a democracy is that which opens the avenues of mutual comprehension, and increases the common ground of humanity. It broadens and harmonizes men on the basis of that which belongs to all mankind. If it elevates certain persons above their fellows, it does not therefore separate them from the race, but joins them to it more broadly. It lifts them as the peaks of a mountain-range are lifted, with a force that spreads the base while it raises the summit. The peaks are the unifying centres of the system. And the springs that rise among the loftiest hills flow down joyfully through the valleys and the plains.

The right ideal of education in a democracy is the creative ideal. It does not seek to adorn men with certain rare accomplishments which shall be the marks of a Brahminical caste. It does not seek to train men for certain practical pursuits with an eye single to their own advantage. It seeks, by a vital culture, to create new men, and new kinds of men, who shall be of ever-increasing worth to the republic and to mankind.

Creation, as it is now interpreted, is a process of development. If this interpretation be true, the result is none the less creative. Species originate, whether their origin be swift or slow.

Education is the human analogue of creation. Its beginning is the unfolding of something which already exists. But its aim, its motive, its triumphant result, is the production of something which did not exist before.

The educated man is a new man. It is not merely that he knows more. It is not merely that he can do more. There is something in him which was not there when his education began. And this something gives him a new relation to the past, of which it is the fruit, and to the future, of which it is the promise. It is of the nature of an original force which draws its energy from a new contact with the world and with mankind, and which distributes its power throughout life in all its channels.

This, it seems to me, is the real object and the right result of education; to create out of the raw stuff that is hidden in the boy a finer, stronger, broader, nobler type of man.

In using this language I am not dealing in glittering generalities. The better manhood of which I speak as the aim of education is no vague and nebulous thing—the dim delight of sensational preachers and virile novelists. It has four definite marks: the power to see clearly, the power to imagine vividly, the power to think independently, and the power to will nobly. These are the objects that the creative ideal sets before us, and in so doing it gives us a standard for all educational effort, from the kindergarten to the university; a measure of what is valuable in old systems and of what is desirable in new theories; and a test of true success in teaching and learning.

I care not whether a man is called a tutor, an instructor, or a full professor; nor whether any academic degrees adorn his name; nor how many facts or symbols of facts he has stored away in his brain. If he has these four powers —clear sight, quick imagination, sound reason, and right, strong will—I call him an educated man and fit to be a teacher.

I use the word "sight" to denote all those senses which are the natural inlets of knowledge. Most men are born with five, but comparatively few learn the use of even one. The majority of people are like the idols described by the psalmist: "Eyes have they, but they see not: they have ears, but they hear not: noses have they, but they smell not." They walk through the world like blind men at a panorama, and find it very dull. There is a story of an Englishwoman who once said to the great painter Turner, by way of comment on one of his pictures: "I never saw anything like that in nature." "Madam," said he, "what would you give if you could?"

The power to use the senses to their full capacity, clearly, sensitively, penetratingly, does not come by nature. It is the fruit of an attentive habit of veracious perception. Such a habit is the result of instruction applied to the opening of blind eyes and the unsealing of deaf ears. The academic studies which have most influence in this direction are those which deal principally with objective facts, such as nature-study, language, numbers, drawing, and music.

But the education of perceptive power is not, and cannot be, carried on exclusively in the study and the class-room. Every meadow and every woodland is a college, and every city square is full of teachers. Do you know how the stream flows, how the kingfisher poises

above it, how the trout swims in it, how the
ferns uncurl along its banks? Do you know
how the human body balances itself, and along
what lines and curves it moves in walking, in
running, in dancing, and in what living characters the thoughts and feelings are written
on the human face? Do you know the struc-
tural aspect of man's temples and palaces and
bridges, of nature's mountains and trees and
flowers? Do you know the tones and accents
of human speech, the songs of birds, the voices
of the forests and the sea? If not, you need
creative culture to make you a sensitive pos-
sessor of the beauty of the world.

Every true university should make room in
its scheme for life out-of-doors. There is much
to be said for John Milton's plan of a school
whose pupils should go together each year on
long horseback journeys and sailing cruises in
order to see the world. Walter Bagehot said
of Shakespeare that he could not walk down
a street without knowing what was in it. John
Burroughs has a college on a little farm beside
the Hudson; and John Muir has a university
called Yosemite. If such men cross a field or
a thicket they see more than the seven wonders
of the world. That is culture. And without it,
all scholastic learning is arid, and all the aca-

demic degrees known to man are but china
oranges hung on a dry tree.

But beyond the world of outward perception
there is another world of inward vision, and
the key to it is imagination. To see things as
they are—that is a precious gift. To see things
as they were in their beginning, or as they will
be in their ending, or as they ought to be in
their perfecting; to make the absent, present;
to rebuild the past out of a fragment of carven
stone; to foresee the future harvest in the grain
of wheat in the sower's hand; to visualise the
face of the invisible, and enter into the lives
of all sorts and conditions of unknown men—
that is a far more precious gift.

Imagination is more than a pleasant fountain; it is a fertilizing stream. Nothing great
has ever been discovered or invented without
the aid of imagination. It is the medium of
all human sympathy. No man can feel with
another unless he can imagine himself in the
other man's place.

The chief instrument in the education of
imagination is literature. The object of literary culture is very simple. It is to teach a
man to distinguish the best books, and to enable him to read them with inward vision. The
man who has read one great book in that way

has become a new creature and entered a new world. But in how many schools and colleges does that ideal prevail? We are spending infinite toil and money to produce spellers and parsers and scanners. We are trying hard to increase the number of people who can write with ease, while the race of people who can read with imagination is left to the care of chance. I wish that we might reverse the process. If our education would but create a race of readers, earnest, intelligent, capable of true imaginative effort, then the old writers would not be forgotten, and the new ones would get a wiser welcome when they arrive.

But the design of education is not accomplished unless a man passes beyond the power of seeing things as they are, and beyond the power of interpreting and appreciating the thoughts of other men, into the power of thinking for himself. To be able to ask, "Why?" and to discover what it means to say, "Because"—that is the intellectual triumph of education.

"To know the best that has been thought and said in the world," is what Matthew Arnold calls culture. It is an excellent attainment. But there is a step beyond it, that leads from culture into manhood. That step is taken when the student, knowing something of the best that other men have thought and said, begins to think his own thoughts clearly through and to put them into his own words. Then he passes through instruction into education. Then he becomes a real person in the intellectual world.

The mere pursuit of knowledge is not necessarily an emancipating thing. There is a kind of reading which is as passive as massage. There is a kind of study which fattens the mind for examination like a prize pig for a county fair. No doubt the beginning of instruction must lie chiefly in exercises of perception and memory. But at a certain point the reason and the judgment must be awakened and brought into voluntary play. As a teacher I would far rather have a pupil give an incorrect answer in a way which showed that he had really been thinking about the subject, than a literally correct answer in a way which showed that he had merely swallowed what I had told him, and regurgitated it on the examination paper.

It seems to me, then, that a teacher should give his pupils rules in such a form that they can use them to work out their own problems. He should instruct them in languages so that words may serve to express clearly and accurately their own thoughts. He should teach them science in order that they may form habits of accurate observation, careful induction, and moderate statement of laws which are not yet fully understood. And if his instruction goes on to philosophy, history, literature, jurisprudence, government, his aim should be to give his pupils some standards by which they can estimate the works and ways, the promises and proposals of men to-day. Pupils thus educated will come out into the world prepared to take a real part in its life. They will be able to form an opinion without waiting for an editorial in their favourite newspaper. They will not need to borrow another man's spectacles before they can trust their eyes.

"My mind to me a kingdom is,"

wrote the quaint old courtly poet, Sir Edward Dyer. But how many there are, in all classes of society, who have no right to use his words. Discrowned monarchs, exiled and landless, desolate and impotent, wearied with trivial cares and dull amusements, enslaved to masters whom they despise and tasks which promise much and pay little—what possession is there that they can call their own, what moment of time in

which they are not at the beck and call of other
men, either grinding stolidly at their round
in the treadmill or dancing idiotically to the
uncomprehended music of some stranger's pipe?
We often say of one whom we wish to blame
slightly and to half excuse, "He is only thoughtless." But there is no deeper word of censure
and reproach in human speech, for it signifies
one who has renounced a rightful dominion
and despised a kindly diadem.

The great dream of education as a loyalist
of the democracy is that "the king shall have
his own again"—that no prince or princess of
the blood royal of humanity shall be self-exiled
in the desert of thoughtlessness or chained in
the slavery of ignorance. A lofty dream, a
distant dream, it may be, but the only way
toward its fulfilment lies through the awaken-
ing of the reason. Not to leave the people in
a dull servitude of groping instincts, while the
chosen few look down on them from the cold
heights of philosophy; but to diffuse through
all the ranks of society an ever-increasing light
of quiet, steady thought on the meaning and
the laws of life—that is the democratic ideal.
Slowly or swiftly we may work toward it, but
only along that line will the people win their
heritage and keep it: the power of self-rule,
through self-knowledge, for the good of all.

CREATIVE EDUCATION

But one more factor is included in the creative ideal of education, and that is its effect upon the will. The power to see clearly, to imagine vividly, to think independently, will certainly be wasted, will be shut up in the individual and kept for his own selfish delight, unless the power to will nobly comes to call the man into action and gives him, with all his education, to the service of the world.

An educated man is helpless until he is emancipated. An emancipated man is aimless until he is consecrated. Consecration is simply concentration, plus a sense of duty.

The final result of true education is not a selfish scholar, nor a scornful critic of the universe, but an intelligent and faithful citizen who is determined to put all his powers at the service of his country and mankind.

What part are our colleges and universities to play in the realizing of this ideal of creative education? Their true function is not exclusive, but inclusive. They are to hold this standard of manhood steadily before them, and recognise its supreme and universal value wherever it is found.

Some of the most thoughtful men in the country have not been college-bred. The university that assumes to look down on these men is false to its own ideal. It should honour them, and learn from them whatever they have to teach. College education is not to be separated from the educative work which pervades the whole social organism. What we need at present is not new colleges with a power of conferring degrees, but more power in the existing colleges to make men. To this end let them have a richer endowment, a fuller equipment, but, above all, a revival of the creative ideal. And let everything be done to bring together the high school, the normal school, the grammar school, the primary school, and the "little-red-schoolhouse" school, in the harmony of this ideal. The university shall still stand in the place of honour, if you will, but only because it bears the clearest and most steadfast witness that the end of education is to create men who can see clearly, imagine vividly, think steadily, and will nobly.

XIV

TEACHING ENGLISH IN SCHOOLS *

IN the ideal America, when all the proposed reforms have been accomplished and the golden, (or near-golden,) age has come, it will perhaps not be necessary to teach English in schools. Children will imbibe it with their sterilized milk, and assimilate it with their digestive food tablets. The newsboys will shout it on the streets, and the newspapers will use it in their headlines. Even the preachers and the lawyers will begin to employ it in their professional duties, and popular authors will write it for the magazines. Readers will naturally select the best books by the instinct of democracy, and a referendum every year will decide what volumes are worthy to survive. The others, being printed on modern acidulated wood-pulp paper will fade away by chemical dissolution. All the bad writers will starve, or be supported in sausage-factories at the expense of the state. Everybody will speak with the same accent and spell in the same way—the shortest way, of

* An address before the New Jersey State Teachers' Association, Atlantic City, December 16, 1912.

217

course, which must always remain the same when once you have found it. When that comes to pass everybody will pronounce and spell correctly, for authority comes from usage, and the usage will be universal, democratic, and therefore infallible. In that age of rolled gold, "English-as-she-is-spoke-and-wrote" will teach herself, and all will go as merry as a telephone bell or an automobile horn.

But those pleasant times, though promised, are remote; and in the real America it appears that there is still great need of teaching English in schools. Indeed the need seems greater and more urgent than it has ever been. Our rich and powerful language is exposed today to dangers of disorder and decay. Our noble literature is in peril from an avalanche of printed stuff which has neither beauty of form nor value of substance, and which threatens to bury all standards of excellence under a mass of mediocrity, and leave the average reader without the wish or the power to distinguish good work from bad.

Consider only a few of these dangers which are acute in the present time.

First, there is the fact—in itself a joyful and hopeful fact, as I look at it—that myriads of children are coming into our schools for whom

TEACHING ENGLISH IN SCHOOLS

English is not the mother-tongue. If they are not taught how to use it well, they will be sure to use it ill; and our national language will be no longer a stately and vigorous tongue which has moulded by its own genius the elements drawn from different sources, but a thing of shreds and patches, invertebrate, shapeless, a poor liquid hodge-podge, like the *lingua franca*, or Pidgin-English.

Then, there is the domineering and tyrannical behaviour of slang in these latter days. Now slang, which is a kind of rough metaphor in the making, is a very useful thing in its place. It is a child bringing in from the shores of life a basket full of all sorts of curiosities, pebbles and shells, weeds and flowers: and every now and then there is something valuable in the miscellany. The really intelligent, picturesque, graphic slang-word of the past often becomes a useful, almost necessary part of the language. "Slang" itself is an example, and "buncombe" is another, and "prig" is another, and "Puritan" is another. There are many words which were once slang, which have now become useful and proper and necessary in the English language. But when the use of slang becomes conventional and thoughtless, a mere nervous habit, an affectation of rough-and-ready vul-

IDEALS AND APPLICATIONS

garity,—when it injects itself into every conversation and sprinkles its senseless phrases over every page like splashes of mud on a clean dress just to give it a free-and-easy air,—then slang becomes a nuisance, because it impoverishes and debases the language. The children who form this habit will lose the power of real self-expression, and the writers who cultivate this vice will become unintelligible as soon as their particular brand of slang goes out of fashion.

A third danger is the reckless disregard of rule and order, of measure and proportion, in the writing of English, which some authors show in their strained efforts to produce sensational effects, and not only to surprise their readers with something new but to shock them with something terrible. Let us take a certain Mr. Thomas W. Lawson (*stet nominis umbra,*) as a near-brazen type of these writers. He puts his words together like strings of firecrackers, intended only for explosion. He fills his paragraphs with hot air like balloons. He exaggerates all that he touches, and shrieks everything that he says. He rushes and roars through the English language like a bull on the rampage, and the fragments lie behind him in ruinous disorder. There are many others like him; and I do not see how it is pos-

sible to read the stuff which they put forth
month after month, without losing the sense of
discrimination, the faculty of enjoying fitness
in words and truth in ideas, and the sincere
and thoughtful love of what is clear and strong
and self-controlled in literature.

There is need, special need in this age of ours,
that the schools should teach English. I will
go further and say that in my opinion it ought
to be the most important, the most interesting,
and the most popular subject of our common
school teaching.

It looks, also, as if it might be an easy subject to teach. But, as a fact, we find by experience that it is not. Perhaps this is because it seems so easy that we do not take pains
to learn how to do it well. Perhaps it is because there are more adverse influences at work,
(and more actively and closely at work,) here
than in other subjects. For example, false
arithmetic is not used in the homes, the shops,
the streets where our pupils spend so much of
their time. But bad English is: teachers of English have to row against a heavy tide. Perhaps
part of our disadvantage arises from the fact
that we have not carefully enough considered
the real aim of teaching English in the schools,
and adjusted our methods to meet it.

IDEALS AND APPLICATIONS

There is a certain part of the instruction in English which must be like the beginning of all other studies,—an exercise of memory, the statement of rules which must be accepted and followed whether the pupil likes them or not. You do not ask your pupils whether they think that Germany should be west of France or east of it. You do not inquire whether they would prefer to have twice three make six or seven. Neither should you ask whether it pleases them to spell "lily" with two l's or with three; or whether their ardent young minds approve of making the verb agree in number with its substantive. The alphabet, and the rules of spelling, and grammar are not matters of preference. They are not subject to the referendum. Children must take them and learn them and apply them to their proper uses. No doubt this involves a good deal of hard and rather disagreeable work; but the more thoroughly and carefully it is done at the beginning the more pleasant and rewarding will be the subsequent study of English.

Once this preliminary labour is passed, English ought to be the most free and flexible and attractive of all the courses in a well-ordered school. Hard and fast systems of teaching it should be distrusted. The "laboratory method of teaching English," (so-called) is an absurdity.

TEACHING ENGLISH IN SCHOOLS

A perfect illustration of it once came to my notice in a certain university. I had gone there to give a single lecture, and after it was done, I went up to spend the evening in a friendly student's room. "What are you doing in English now?" "Oh," he answered, "we are specializing on the style of R. L. Stevenson." "That is interesting," I said; "and how do you like it?" "Pretty good," replied my student, "pretty good! But he ain't up to O. Henry or Harold Bell Wright." This reply stimulated my curiosity, and I pursued the subject by making another inquiry: "What method are you following in your study of Stevenson's style?" "The laboratory method," replied my student promptly; "we are getting his number on the Anglo-Saxon words he uses, compared with the Latin words." "Would you mind telling me," I asked, "just how you arrive at your computation?" "Sure," replied my student cheerfully; "the Prof has told me to take this book," (here he showed me a copy of *The Wrong Box*,) "and told me to count the number of words which come out of Anglo-Saxon, and the number which come out of Latin, in fifty pages. Then I work out the percentage of each, and get the result."

My wonder at this simple method of teaching English could not be expressed. It would

have been vain to point out to my young friend
the fact that *The Wrong Box* was not written
by Stevenson alone, but mainly by his collab-
orator Lloyd Osbourne. It would have been
superfluous to suggest that you can no more
get at the secret of a fine style by counting the
relative number of words of Saxon and of Latin
origin, than you can discover the magic of Titian
as a colourist by finding out what kind of oil
he used to mix his paints with. In fact there
was only one thing that you could have done,
(with any chance of success,) to save that
poor student from the "ignorance of the
learned," as Hazlitt calls it. You could have
read to the ingenuous young man a few pages
of *Markheim*, or *Will o' the Mill*, or *A Gossip
on Romance*, and then perhaps,—if you had
any notion how to read aloud,—that young
man might have perceived a glimmer of the
charm of Stevenson's style.

Words are not atoms; nor are books chemical compounds. The vital, practical, literary
method is the only one that is appropriate in
teaching English; and that is a method that
varies and changes with the needs of the pupils
and the capacities of the teacher. The essential
thing is to have clearly in mind the real purpose, the final goal of the English course in
schools and colleges.

TEACHING ENGLISH IN SCHOOLS

And what is that?

Certainly it is not to make authors.

In the first place, that would be impossible. It is not within the power of any school or college to make a master of English literature. That subtle balance of the powers of thought and feeling, that sensitive perception of the value and colour of words, that combination of intelligence and imagination, of reason and emotion, which gives a man something to say and the faculty of saying it so that it shall be memorable, is not to be conferred by academies or courses of instruction. It is a gift. It is on the lap of the Gods. Even if it were possible, how cruel it would be to manufacture all the boys and girls in our schools into writers and teach them to look forward to making their living with the pen! The world could not support so many authors. The flood of books would be intolerable, and the magazine editors would be driven to desperation.

No; what we aim at in teaching English, if I think rightly about it, is something much simpler, and, upon the whole, much more admirable and useful than making authors. It is, first, to train children to find more pleasure and profit in the reading of good books; and second, to teach them to use their own language for the ordinary purposes of life, with intelligence, clearness, precision, and force. That is the whole of it.

As far as English is concerned, the scholar who comes out of school able to find pleasure and profit in the reading of good books and able to express himself with clearness, intelligence, precision, and force in the ordinary affairs of life, is educated in English. In other words, the object of the teaching of English in our schools is to bring up men and women who shall be able to enjoy what they read and to know why they enjoy it, and to say what they mean and to say it well. How many are there who come up to this simple standard?

Reading, then, is one part of our English course, and self-expression in writing and speaking is the other. They should always be closely related because they help each other. They should be carried forward side by side, and yet they may be considered separately.

First, then, in regard to reading. For the books to be used in the earlier stages of the study of English, I should always choose those which have a natural interest for the young. They should have a direct and straightforward style, and a subject closely related to life. Nothing could be better for the purpose than such stories of adventure as *Robinson Crusoe* and *Treasure Island*, or such fairy-tales as the

Jungle Books of Rudyard Kipling—professedly realistic, but actually the very extreme of idealism. Washington Irving's stories, and Hawthorne's, and Poe's tales, and Cooper's novels—more particularly, I think, *The Spy*, which seems to me the best suited for this purpose,—all these are good stuff. The story is the chief thing for the young mind. Maybe it ought not to be so, but you cannot change it.

Along with the story the teacher should try to bring out the characters which are concerned in it. What effect do they have upon the development of the plot? Would it change the story if they were different? If you put Brom Bones into "Rip Van Winkle," would the story change? I think it would. Do the characters grow better or worse? Do they change in any way as the plot unfolds, or are they like those little Italian marionettes that are made out of wood, a villain always villainous and a hero always heroic? In reading a book, I would try to suggest to the pupil's mind the natural characteristics of the persons and the significance of the events through which they passed; and if by any chance the book proved to be so dead that I could not do this, I would cut it out of the course, and take another book.

For the most part, I prefer books about other times and other scenes from those in which my pupils are now living. "Looking-glass fiction" is not particularly good for boys and girls; it does not enlarge their horizon enough. Far better than reading about little Susie and her parties, or young Mike and his baseball team, is it for them to read stories of high achievement and romantic adventure. They themselves will take the part of the knights and ladies who please them. There is something of the hero in every boy; something of the heroine in every girl; and reading is one way to get at it and wake it up.

I would not shirk or evade the moral lesson of the book. Great authors have almost always meant to teach something by their writings. But their way of teaching is distinct and peculiar. They have not intended to teach as catechists, by definition of theological or ethical doctrines. Whenever they have done that, they have failed. They have not meant to teach as preachers, exhorting men to virtue and good conduct, although, occasionally, some of the very greatest, like Thackeray, come very near to preaching. They have intended to teach as artists. The real artist conveys his moral teaching in the vital sap, in the animating spirit of his work. You may receive it from any part of the story, and it does not need to be put into italics at the end, after the manner of the moral of one of Æsop's *Fables*.

The best writers have always wished their works to signify something in the way of counsel for human life, and as they called their characters into being and led them through their adventures, they meant that they should say something to us, and tell us something about this world, and about the paths which lead through it, whether to glory or to despair. True art teaches just as life itself teaches, because true art is a reflection of life, an image and interpretation of life, and the meaning and significance of life is in it. Do not hesitate, therefore, to say for yourself and to ask your pupils to say for themselves, what they fancy is the meaning of such and such a book that they have read, and what it seems to say to them about the best way to live. Above all, do not hesitate to ask them, Does it leave you with more courage, or with less; does it leave you with more desire to do the right, or with less?

"Comparative Literature" is not for schools. It is for universities and post-graduate work. Positive literature is the thing to begin with. "You do not want," Mr. Moody once said, "to discuss the question whether there were two, or

three, Isaiahs with people who don't know that
there was one." You only spoil boys and girls
if you try to make comparative critics out of
them. They have to unlearn it all when they
get to the university. They have not breadth
of mind enough. They have not sufficient
standards of judgment for this kind of work.
Give them good books and let them read them
for the pleasure of it; and then help them to
understand the pleasure and to deepen it.
Even with great books: Shakespeare, Milton,
Scott, Thackeray, if you bring them into the
school, do it simply; cut out the elaborate notes.
Almost all our text-books are over-annotated.
Cut out the comparisons with other world-
masters. Cut out curious investigations of
literary sources and origins. Those are not
for boys and girls, but for mature students.
Let Hamlet's story, or Othello's, be the central
thing. Children of fifteen and sixteen can ap-
preciate those stories; can get at least an outline of them. Let the story be the chief, the
central thing, and then try to make it so real,
so living, that the words of Hamlet and of
Othello shall be memorable, and that your
pupils shall understand what they mean as
coming out of the life and the tragedy of that
particular story.

TEACHING ENGLISH IN SCHOOLS

Of poetry, I should use those examples in which the narrative interest predominates: ballads of Longfellow and Whittier, of Wordsworth and Tennyson; little epics of Scott and Byron; *The Ancient Mariner* of Coleridge is one of the best poems in the world to teach young pupils. Lowell's *Vision of Sir Launfal* is another beautiful thing, perfect in its kind. These are all excellent. No matter what the academic and anæmic critics may say to you about Longfellow and Whittier, they are poets who interpret life through the imagination in the terms of music and emotion. That is what it is to be a poet. Beginning with these smaller things, I should go on to larger things, like Tennyson's *Idylls of the King*, and some of Browning's dramatic lyrics. But I should not begin Browning too soon in the teaching of poetry, lest the pupil should become discouraged. Browning is, in the main, rather difficult, and should be kept, I think, for the later years. I should practice much the habit of reading aloud, and if I didn't know how to do it, I should try to learn.

Poetry is meant to be heard, not seen. The real word is not a printed word, nor a written word; it is a spoken word. Half the power of poetry depends upon its music, its rhythm and flow, its cadence and its sonority or sweetness.

IDEALS AND APPLICATIONS

How can you expect children really to like it unless you give it to them in the fullness of its power and with all that belongs to it, in form as well as in substance? Not only should we read poetry to them, and read it as well as we can, but also we should ask them to read poetry to us, and we should listen carefully to see whether they have cleansed their voices, as well as washed their faces; whether they have learned to speak in a tone which really expresses what is best in them; and whether they follow the feeling of the poem and go along with it. If you will try that method of teaching, and try it over, and over, and over again, you will find that the children will learn to love poetry.

People say, "I don't care for poetry," just as if they were saying, "I don't care for caviar." But to say, "I don't care for poetry" is like saying, "I don't care for sunlight or pure air! I don't care for the mountains, and I don't care for the sea!" Why don't you care for poetry? Who lamed you, who crippled you, who blinded you, who took away your hearing for the music and the sweet harmony of thought and feeling which have flowed into the poetry of the ages? Not care for poetry? It is a confession that one ought to be ashamed of. Everybody ought to care for poetry; not everybody for the same kind of poetry, but everybody for some kind of poetry. Everybody—man, woman, and child—ought to care for having the experiences in life lifted up, transfigured and illuminated by that "light that never was on sea or land."

Try, when you read poetry, to give not only the *sense* of the words, but to call also the attention of your children to the *suggestion* of the words. It is wonderful. I always remember, in this connection, a line of Wordsworth. It is in one of the inscriptions that he wrote for the naming of places:

> "*There is an eminence of these our hills.*
> *The last that* parleys *with the setting sun,*"

How magical is that word "parleys," with its suggestion of the mountain speaking its farewell to the sun, and the sun sending back its "we meet again" to the mountain, irradiated with the last rosy glow. If you have made a boy or girl understand the meaning of that word "parley" in this poem, you have opened a new world. You have made life richer and more beautiful for that child.

Of that part of English teaching which has to do with speaking and writing, I have less to say, because I know less about it. Only one thing I venture to affirm absolutely and without qualification; no method of teaching composition is good which makes the pupils write either with unnatural stiffness or with slovenly indifference. Every method is good which cultivates freedom and precision at the same time.

Writing good English is like playing golf. Any one who has played golf successfully will tell you that the first thing you must get is *good form*. There are certain things you must not do; but after you have got your good form, you must get a free swing; you must keep your eye on the ball and you must "follow through." I do not know that I could give any better advice about writing English than that. Get good form, then swing free, keep your eye on the ball, and follow through.

I do not believe in the "daily theme" as a method of teaching composition. In the first place, I think it puts more work upon the teacher than any teacher can conscientiously do. In the second place, I think it is thoroughly unnatural; it has no relation to anything that the pupils are likely to be called upon to do afterward in life. The only persons that I know in actual life who have to write a daily theme are the newspaper editors; and for that they have a long and special training, and they themselves will tell you that this training cannot be given anywhere outside of a newspaper office. I think they are right. Perhaps there is one other class that has to write a daily theme, and that class is composed of persons who have just become engaged to be married. When they are separated, they are under the necessity of writing a daily theme, but the schools do not need to take any trouble about that; nature will attend to it. I think that a far better way than the daily theme is to have a weekly or fortnightly theme. There are a good many useful methods of getting that out of the pupils, and one I have found most useful is to read a poem or story to a group of students and then ask them afterward, without referring to the book at all, to write in a few words their own version of the core and kernel of the poem or story.

All through the teaching of composition, I would call attention to the fact that words are living things; that they have their histories, their associations, their atmosphere, their colour. I would try to teach my pupils not to say "suspect" when they mean "expect," not to use "ride" for "drive," and not to think that "to transpire" means "to happen." I would show them that the charm and power of a great book depend upon just this respect for words, this insight into their meaning, this delicate sense of their finely shaded significance. It is a great joy to find the right word when you have been looking for it a long time. It is like coming upon a hidden treasure. In regard to the use of words, I think the formal rules of rhetoric are of little value compared with the power of example and imitation, and I think almost all good writers of English have learned to write by copying somebody.

Thus I have expressed, (or confessed,) my views and persuasions concerning the teaching of English in schools, and the two factors which enter into it—reading and writing. However lightly and imperfectly I have touched the subject, my conviction of its importance is profound. We are in perilous times to-day for the purity of the English language and for the standards of English literature. They are shaken on every side, and there are few indeed to hold them up faithfully. Who shall do it? Who can do it better than the teachers in our schools? Stand firm, and win people by your teaching and by your example to a deeper reverence for our rich and noble English tongue.

TEACHING ENGLISH IN SCHOOLS

So will you rally those who will help to preserve it from debasement. Strive to increase the love of the children for our splendid and inspiring literature. So will you enlarge and enrich the lives of those who are to be the makers of the America that is to come.

XV

THE SCHOOL OF LIFE *

MANY fine things have been said in commencement addresses about "Culture and Progress," "The Higher Learning," "American Scholarship," "The University Spirit," "The Woman's College," and other subjects bearing on the relation of education to life. But the most important thing, after all,—the thing which needs not only to be said, but also to be understood,—is that life itself is the great school.

This whole framework of things visible and invisible wherein we mysteriously find ourselves perceiving, reasoning, reflecting, desiring, choosing, and acting, is designed and fitted, so far at least as it concerns us and reveals itself to us, to be a place of training and enlightenment for the human race through the unfolding and development of human persons such as you and me.

For no other purpose are these wondrous

* Commencement address, Smith College, Northampton, Massachusetts, June 21, 1904.

potencies of perception and emotion, thought and will, housed within walls of flesh and shut in by doors of sense, but that we may learn to set them free and lead them out. For no other purpose are we beset with attractions and repulsions, obstacles and allurements, tasks, duties, pleasures, persons, books, machines, plants, animals, houses, forests, storm and sunshine, water fresh and salt, fire wild and tame, a various earth, a mutable heaven, and an intricate humanity, but that we may be instructed in the nature of things and people, and rise by knowledge and sympathy, through gradual and secret promotions, into a fuller and finer life.

Facts are teachers. Experiences are lessons. Friends are guides. Work is a master. Love is an interpreter. Teaching itself is a method of learning. Joy carries a divining rod and discovers fountains. Sorrow is an astronomer and shows us the stars.

What I have lived I really know, and what I really know I partly own; and so, begirt with what I know and what I own, I move through my curriculum, elective and required, gaining nothing but what I learn, at once instructed and examined by every duty and every pleasure.

It is a mistake to say, "To-day education ends, to-morrow life begins." The process is continuous: the idea into the purpose, the purpose into the action, the action into the character. When the mulberry seed falls into the ground and germinates, it begins to be transformed into silk.

This view of life as a process of education was held by the Greeks and the Hebrews—the two races in whose deep hearts the stream of modern progress takes its rise, the two great races whose energy of spirit and strength of self-restraint have kept the world from sinking into the dream-lit torpor of the mystic East, or whirling into the blind, restless activity of the barbarian West.

What is it but the idea of the school of life that sings through the words of the Hebrew psalmist? "I will instruct thee and teach thee in the way which thou shalt go. I will guide thee with mine eye. Be ye not as the horse or as the mule, whose mouth must be held in with bit and bridle lest they come near unto thee." This warning against the mulish attitude which turns life into a process of punishment, this praise of the eye-method which is the triumph of teaching—these are the notes of a wonderful and world-wide school.

It is the same view of life that shines through Plato's noble words: "This then must be our notion of the just man, that even when he is in poverty or sickness, or any other seeming misfortune, all things will in the end work together for good to him in life and death; for the gods have a care of anyone whose desire is to become just, and to be like God, as far as man can attain his likeness by the pursuit of virtue."

Not always, indeed, did the Greek use so strong an ethical emphasis. For him the dominant idea was the unfolding of reason, the clarifying of the powers of thought and imagination. His ideal man was one who saw things as they are, and understood their nature, and felt beauty, and followed truth.

It was the Hebrew who laid the heavier stress upon the conception of righteousness. The foundations of his school were the tablets on which the divine laws, "Thou shalt" and "Thou shalt not," were inscribed. The ideal of his education was the power to distinguish between good and evil, and the will to choose the good, and the strength to stand by it. Life, to his apprehension, fulfilled its purpose in the development of a man who walked uprightly and kept the commandments.

Thus these two master-races of antiquity, alike in their apprehension of existence from

IDEALS AND APPLICATIONS

the standpoint of the soul, worked out their thought of vital education, along the lines of different temperaments, to noble results. Æschylus and Ezekiel lived in the same century.

Reason and Righteousness: what more can the process of life do to justify itself than to unfold these two splendid flowers on the tree of our humanity? What third idea is there that the third great race, the Anglo-Saxon, may conceive, and cherish, and bring to blossom and fruition?

There is only one—the idea of Service. Too much the sweet reasonableness of the Greek ideal tended to foster an intellectual isolation; too much the strenuous righteousness of the Hebrew ideal gave shelter to the microbe of Pharisaism. It was left for the Anglo-Saxon race, quickened by the new word and the new life of a divine Teacher, to claim for the seed an equal glory with the flower and the fruit; to perceive that righteousness is not reasonable, and reason is not righteous, unless they are both communicable and serviceable; to say that the highest result of our human experience is to bring forth better men and women, able and willing to give of that which makes them better to the world in which they live.

THE SCHOOL OF LIFE

This is the ultimate word concerning the school of life. I catch its inspiring note in the question of that very noble gentleman, Sir Philip Sidney, who said: "To what purpose should our thoughts be directed to various kinds of knowledge, unless room be afforded for putting it into practice, so that public advantage may be the result?" These then are what the education of life is to bring out—Reason, Righteousness, and Service.

But if life itself be the school, what becomes of our colleges and universities? They are, or they ought to be, simply preparatory institutions to fit us to go on with our education. Not what do they teach, but how do they prepare us to learn—that is the question. I measure a college not by the height of its towers, nor by the length of its examination papers, nor by the pride of its professors, but chiefly by the docility of its graduates. I do not ask, Where did you leave off? but, Are you ready to go on? Graduation is not a stepping out; it is either a stepping up—*gradu ad gradum*—a promotion to a higher class, or a dropping to a lower one. The cause for which a student is dropped may be invincible ignorance, incurable frivolity, or obstructive and constrictive learning.

"One of the benefits of a college education,"

says Emerson, "is to show a boy its little avail." Hamilton and Jefferson and Madison and Adams and Webster were college men. But Franklin, Washington, Marshall, Clay, and Lincoln were not.

A college education is good for those who can digest it. The academic atmosphere has its dangers, of which the greatest are a certain illusion of infallibility, a certain fever of intellectual jealousy, and a certain dry idolatry of schedules and programmes. But these infirmities hardly touch the mass of students, busy as they are nowadays with their athletics, their societies, their youthful pleasures. The few who are affected more seriously are usually cured by contact with the larger world. Most of the chronic cases occur among those who really never leave the preparatory institution, but pass from the class to the instructor's seat, and from that to the professorial chair, and so along the spiral, bounded ever by the same curve and steadily narrowing inward.

Specialists we must have; and to-day we are told that a successful specialist must give his whole life to the study of the viscosity of electricity, or the value of the participial infinitive, or some such pin-point of concentration. For this a secluded and cloistered life may be necessary. But let us have room also in our colleges for teachers who have been out in the world, and touched life on different sides, and taken part in various labours, and been buffeted, and learned how other men live, and what troubles them, and what they need. Great is the specialist, and precious; but I think we still have a use for masters of the old type, who knew many things, and were broadened by experience, and had the power of vital inspiration, and could start their pupils on and up through the struggles and triumphs of a lifelong education.

There is much discussion nowadays of the subjects which may be, or must be, taught in a college. A part, at least, of the controversy is futile. For the main problem is not one of subjects, but of aim and method. "Liberal studies," says Professor S. H. Butcher, one of the finest modern teachers of Greek, "pursued in an illiberal spirit, fall below the mechanical arts in dignity and worth." There are two ways of teaching any subject: one opens the mind, the other closes it.

The mastery of the way to do things is the accomplishment that counts for future work. I like the teacher who shows me not merely where he stands, but how he got there, and who encourages and equips me to find my own path through the maze of books and the tangled thickets of human opinion.

Let us keep our colleges and universities true to their function, which is preparatory and not final. Let us not ask of them a yearly output of "finished scholars." The very phrase has a mortuary sound, like an epitaph. He who can learn no more has not really learned anything. What we want is not finished scholars, but well-equipped learners; minds that can give and take; intellects not cast in a mould, but masters of a method; people who are ready to go forward wisely toward a larger wisdom.

The chief benefit that a good student may get in a good college is not a definite amount of Greek and Latin, mathematics and chemistry, botany and zoölogy, history and logic, though this in itself is good. But far better is the power to apprehend and distinguish, to weigh evidence and interpret facts, to think clearly, to infer carefully, to imagine vividly. Best of all is a sense of the unity of knowledge, a reverence for the naked truth, a perception of the variety of beauty, a feeling of the significance of literature, and a wider sympathy with the upward-striving, dimly groping, perplexed and dauntless life of man.

THE SCHOOL OF LIFE

I will not ask whether such a result of college training has any commercial value, whether it enables one to command a larger wage in the market-place, whether it opens the door to wealth, or fame, or social distinction; nor even whether it increases the chance of winning a place in the red book of *Who's Who*. These questions are treasonable to the very idea of education, which aims not at a marketable product, but at a vital development. The one thing certain and important is that those who are wisely and liberally disciplined and enlightened in any college enter the school of life with an advantage. They are "well prepared," as we say. They are fitted to go on with their education in reason and righteousness and service under the great Master.

I do not hold with the modern epigram that "the true university is a library." Through the vast wilderness of books flows the slender stream of literature, and often there is need of guidance to find and follow it. Only a genius or an angel can safely be turned loose in a library to wander at will. Nothing is more offensive than the complacent illusion of omniscience begotten in an ignorant person by the haphazard reading of a few volumes of philosophy or science.

IDEALS AND APPLICATIONS

There is a certain kind of reading that is little better than an idle habit, a substitute for thought. Of many books it may be said that they are nothing but the echoes of echoing echoes. If a good book be, as Milton said, "the precious life-blood of a master-spirit, embalmed and treasured," still the sacred relic, as in the phial of St. Januarius at Naples, remains solid and immovable. It needs a kind of miracle to make it liquefy and flow—the miracle of interpretation and inspiration—wrought most often by the living voice of a wise master, and communicating to the young heart the wonderful secret that some books are alive. Never shall I forget the miracle wrought for me by the reading of Milton's *Comus* by my father in his book-lined study on Brooklyn Heights, and of Cicero's *Letters* by Professor Packard in the Latin class at old Princeton.

The Greeks learned the alphabet from the Phœnicians. But the Phœnicians used it for contracts, deeds, bills of lading, and accounts; the Greeks for poetry and philosophy. Contracts and accounts, of all kinds, are for filing. Literature is of one kind only, the interpretation of life and nature through the imagination in clear and personal words of power and charm. And this is for reading.

THE SCHOOL OF LIFE

To get the good of the library in the school of life you must bring into it something better than a mere bookish taste. You must bring the power to read, between the lines, behind the words, beyond the horizon of the printed page. Philip's question to the chamberlain of Ethiopia was crucial: "Understandest thou what thou readest?"

I want books not to pass the time, but to fill it with beautiful thoughts and images, to enlarge my world, to give me new friends in the spirit, to purify my ideals and make them clear, to show me the local colour of unknown regions and the bright stars of universal truth.

Time is wasted if we read too much looking-glass fiction, books about our own class and place and period, stories of American college life, society novels, tales in which our own conversation is repeated and our own prejudices are embodied—Kodak prints, Gramophone cylinders! I prefer the real voice, the visible face, things which I can see and hear for myself without waiting for Miss Arabella Tompkins' report of them. When I read, I wish to go abroad, to hear new messages, to meet new people, to get a fresh point of view, to revisit other ages, to listen to the oracles of Delphi and drink deep of the springs of Pieria. The only writer who can tell me anything of real value about my familiar environment is the genius who shows me that after all it is not familiar, but strange, wonderful, crowded with secrets unguessed and possibilities unrealized.

The two things best worth reading about in poetry and fiction are the symbols of nature and the passions of the human heart. I want also an essayist who will clarify life by gentle illumination and lambent humour; a philosopher who will help me to see the reason of things apparently unreasonable; a historian who will show me how peoples have risen and fallen; and a biographer who will let me touch the hand of the great and the good. This is the magic of literature. This is how real books help to educate us in the school of life.

There is no less virtue, but rather more, in events, tasks, duties, obligations, than there is in books. Work itself has a singular power to unfold and develop our nature. The difference is not between working people and thinking people, but between people who work without thinking and people who think while they work.

What is it that you have to do? To weave cloth, to grow fruit, to sell bread, to make a fire, to prepare food, to nurse the sick, to keep house? It matters not. Your task brings you the first lesson of reason—that you must deal with things as they are, not as you imagine or desire them to be. Wet wood will not burn. Fruit trees must have sunshine. Heavy bread will not sell. Sick people have whims. Empty cupboards yield no dinners. The house will not keep itself. Platitudes, no doubt; but worth more for education than many a metaphysical theory or romantic dream. For when we face these things and realize their meaning, they lead us out of the folly of trying to live in such a world as we would like it to be, and make us live in the world which is.

The mystic visions of the dreamy Orient are a splendid pageant. But for guidance I follow a teacher like Socrates, whose gods were too noble to deceive or masquerade, whose world was a substantial embodiment of divine ideas, and whose men and women were not playthings of Fate or Chance, but living souls, working, struggling, fighting their way to victory.

I do not wish to stay with the nurse and hear fairy tales. I prefer to enter the school of life. In the presence of the mysteries of pain and suffering, under the pressure of disaster or disease, I turn not for counsel to some Scythian soothsayer with her dark incantations and her

251

vague assurances that the evil will vanish if I only close my eyes, but to such a calm, wise teacher as Hippocrates, who says: "As for me, I think that these maladies are divine, like all others, but that none is more divine or more human than another. Each has its natural principle, and none exists without its natural cause."

This is intellectual fortitude. And fortitude is the sentinel and guardian virtue; without it all other virtues are in peril. Daring is inborn, and often born blind. But fortitude is implanted, nurtured, unfolded in the school of life.

I praise the marvellous courage of the human heart, enduring evils, facing perplexities, overcoming obstacles, rising after a hundred falls, building up what gravity pulls down, toiling at tasks never finished, relighting extinguished fires, and hoping all things. I like not the implication of Byron's line—"*fair* women and *brave* men"—for women are not less brave than men, but often more brave, though in a different way. Life itself takes them in hand, these delicate and gracious creatures; and, if they are worthy and willing, true scholars of experience, educates them in a heroism of the heart which suffers all the more splendidly because it is sensitive, and conquers fear all the more gloriously because it is timorous.

The obstinacy of the materials with which we have to deal, in all kinds of human work, has an educational value. Someone has called it "the total depravity of inanimate things." The phrase would be fit if depravity could be conceived of as beneficent.

No doubt a world in which matter never got out of place and became dirt, in which iron had no flaws and wood no cracks, in which gardens had no weeds and food grew ready cooked, in which clothes never wore out and washing was as easy as the soap-makers' advertisements describe it, in which rules had no exceptions and things never went wrong, would be a much easier place to live in. But for purposes of training and development it would be worth nothing at all.

It is the resistance that puts us on our mettle: it is the conquest of the reluctant stuff that educates the worker. I wish you enough difficulties to keep you well and make you strong and skilful!

No one can get the full benefit of the school of life who does not welcome the silent and deep instruction of nature. This earth on which

we live, these heavens above us, these dumb
companions of our work and play, this wondrous
living furniture and blossoming drapery of our
school-room—all have their lessons to impart.
But they will not teach swiftly and suddenly;
they will not let us master their meaning in a
single course, or sum it all up in a single treatise.
Slowly, gradually, with infinite reserves, with
delicate confidences, as if they would prolong
their instruction that we may not forsake their
companionship, they yield up their significance
to the student who loves them.

The scientific study of nature is often com-
mended on merely practical grounds. I would
honour and praise it for higher reasons—for
its power to train the senses in the habit of
veracious observation; for its corrective influence upon the audacity of a logic which would
attempt to evolve the camel from the inner
consciousness of a philosopher; for its steady-
ing, quieting effect upon the mind. Poets have
indulged too often in supercilious sneers at the
man of science, the natural philosopher—

> "a fingering slave,
> One that would peep and botanise
> Upon his mother's grave."

THE SCHOOL OF LIFE

The contempt is ill founded; the sneer is indiscriminate. It is as if one should speak of
the poet as—

> "*A man of trifling breath,*
> *One that would flute and sonneteer*
> *About his sweetheart's death.*"

Is there any more danger of narrowing the
mind by the patient scrutiny of plants and
birds than by the investigation of ancient docu-
ments and annals, or the study of tropes, meta-
phors, and metres? Is it only among men of
science that we find pettiness, and irascibility,
and domineering omniscience, or do they sometimes occur among historians and poets? It
seems to me that there are no more serene and
admirable intelligences than those which are
often found among the true naturalists. How
fine and enviable is their life-long pursuit of
their chosen subject. What mind could be
happier in its kingdom than that of an Agassiz
or a Guyot? What life more beautiful and
satisfying than that of a Linnæus or an Audu-
bon?

But for most of us these advanced courses
in natural science are impossible. What we
must content ourselves with is not really worthy
to be called nature-study; it is simply nature-

kindergarten. We learn a little about the movements of the stars and clouds; a few names of trees and flowers and birds; some of the many secrets of their life and growth; just the words of one syllable, that is all. And then if we are wise and teachable, we walk with Nature, and let her breathe into our hearts those lessons of humility, and patience, and confidence, and good cheer, and tranquil resignation, and temperate joy, which are her "moral lore"—lessons which lead her scholars onward through a merry youth, and a strong maturity, and a serene old age, and prepare them by the pure companionship of this world for the enjoyment of a better.

The social environment, the human contact in all its forms, plays a large part in the school of life. "The city instructs men," said Simonides.

Conversation is an exchange of ideas: this is what distinguishes it from gossip and chatter. The organisation of work, the division of labour, implies and should secure a mutual education of the workers. Some day, when this is better understood, the capitalist will be enlightened and the labour-union civilized.

Even the vexed problem of domestic service is capable of yielding educational results to those who are busy with it. The mistress may learn something of the nature of fair dealing, the responsibilities of command, the essential difference between a carpet-sweeping machine and the girl who pushes it. The servant may learn something of the dignity of doing any kind of work well, the virtue of self-respecting obedience, and the sweet reasonableness of performing the task that is paid for.

I do not think much of the analogy between human society and the bee-hive or the ant-hill, which certain writers are now elaborating in subtle symbolist fashion. It passes over and ignores the vital problem which is ever pressing upon us humans—the problem of reconciling personal claims with the claims of the race. Among the bees and the ants, so far as we can see, the community is all, the individual is nothing. There are no personal aspirations to suppress; no conscious conflicts of duty and desire; no dreams of a better kind of hive, a new and perfected formicary. It is only to repeat themselves, to keep the machine going, to reproduce the same hive, the same ant-hill, that these perfect communisms blindly strive. But human society is less perfect, and therefore more promising. The highest achievements of humanity come from something which, so far as we know, bees and ants do not possess:

the sense of imperfection, the desire of advance.

Ideals must be personal before they can become communal. It was not until the rights of the individual were perceived and recognised, including the right to the pursuit of happiness, that the vision of a free and noble state, capable of progress, dawned upon mankind.

Life teaches all but the obstinate and mean how to find a place in such a state and grow therein. A true love of others is the counterpart of a right love of self; that is, a love for the better part, the finer, nobler self, the man that is

"to arise in me,
That the man that I am may cease to be."

Individualism is a fatal poison. But individuality is the salt of common life. You may have to live in a crowd, but you do not have to live like it, nor subsist on its food. You may have your own orchard. You may drink at a hidden spring. Be yourself if you would serve others.

Learn also how to appraise criticism, to value enmity, to get the good of being blamed and evil spoken of. A soft social life is not likely to be very noble. You can hardly tell whether your faiths and feelings are real until they are attacked.

But take care that you defend them with an open mind and by right reason. You are entitled to a point of view, but not to announce it as the centre of the universe. Prejudice, more than anything else, robs life of its educational value. I knew a man who maintained that the chief obstacle to the triumph of Christianity was the practice of infant baptism. I heard a woman say that no one who ate with his knife could be a gentleman. Hopeless scholars these!

What we call society is very narrow. But life is very broad. It includes "the whole world of God's cheerful, fallible men and women." It is not only the famous people and the well-dressed people who are worth meeting. It is everyone who has something to communicate. The scholar has something to say to me, if he be still alive. But I would hear also the traveller, the manufacturer, the soldier, the good workman, the forester, the village school-teacher, the nurse, the quiet observer, the unspoiled child, the skilful housewife. I knew an old German woman, living in a city tenement, who said: "My heart is a little garden, and God is planting flowers there."

IDEALS AND APPLICATIONS

"*Il faut cultiver son jardin*"—yes, but not only that. One should learn also to enjoy the neighbour's garden, however small; the roses straggling over the fence, the scent of lilacs drifting across the road.

There is a great complaint nowadays about the complication of life, especially in its social and material aspects. It is bewildering, confusing, overstraining. It destroys the temper of tranquillity necessary to education. The simple life is recommended, and rightly, as a refuge from this trouble.

But perhaps we need to understand a little more clearly what simplicity is. It does not consist merely in low ceilings, loose garments, and the absence of *bric-à-brac*. Life may be conventional and artificial in a log cabin. Philistines have their prejudices, and the etiquette of the cotton-mill is often as absurd and burdensome as that of the manor-house.

A little country town, with its inflexible social traditions, its petty animosities and jealousies, its obstinate mistrust of all that is strange, and its crude gossip about all that it cannot comprehend, with its sensitive self-complacency, and its subtle convolutions of parish politics, and its rivalries on a half-inch scale, may be as complicated and as hard to live in as great Babylon itself.

THE SCHOOL OF LIFE

Simplicity depends but little on external things. It can live in broadcloth or homespun; it can eat white bread or black. It is not outward, but inward. A certain openness of mind to learn the daily lessons of the school of life; a certain willingness of heart to give and to receive that extra service, that gift beyond the strict measure of debt, which makes friendship possible; a certain clearness of spirit to perceive the best in things and people, to love it without fear and to cleave to it without mistrust; a peaceable sureness of affection and taste; a gentle straightforwardness of action; a kind sincerity of speech—these are the marks of the simple life. It cometh not with observation, for it is within you. I have seen it in a hut. I have seen it in a palace. And wherever it is found it is the best prize of the school of life, the badge of a scholar well-beloved of the Master.

XVI

TO-MORROW'S MESSAGE TO TO-DAY *

IN the White Palace of Dreams at Washington, the universal station of the super-wireless telephone, there is a certain apartment called the Listening-in Room. There, if you have the proper cap on your head, you may hear the strangest things in the world. That which is whispered in closets sounds as if proclaimed from the house-tops. Engagements not yet made are discussed as promises already half-broken. Kings and Kaisers that were, hold converse with Revolutionists still unhatched. Presidents-to-be appoint their Secretaries and Ambassadors. Cabinets in conjecture select their Presidents. Chambers of Commerce choose their Senators. Labour Leaders distribute wealth and leisure not yet worked for; songs unsung vibrate in the air; and histories of what might have happened play through the narratives of what has oc-

* An address made at the Centenary Celebration of Hawaiian Missions, on Civics Day, April 15, 1920, Honolulu.

curred. Fact and fiction blend, even as they do in real life. Only those who are taught of the Spirit discern the Truth in the midst of the Big Talk.

One conversation which I overheard in that mysterious room has left an indelible impression on my memory. There was a sharp ring of the annunciator bell; then a voice, far-away and slow, but wonderfully clear, began speaking.

"Hello, hello! I want to speak to To-day!"

Then another voice, quick and loud but rather hoarse, as if it had been talking a great deal and was rather cross and tired, replied impatiently:

"Hello there! Here I am,—To-day speaking! I'm very busy. What do you want? Who are you? What's your number?"

The slow, clear voice answered quietly:

"My number is next to yours in the Book. This is To-morrow speaking. I have a message for you."

The voice of To-day broke into a husky laugh.

"O piffle! I never heard such impudence. Why look here, you To-morrow, you don't exist, you're not on the map. How can you talk? Ring off."

"Wait just a minute," answered the voice of

IDEALS AND APPLICATIONS

To-morrow: "I assure you that I am on the everlasting map quite as much as you are. A thousand years from now, people will see us close together, one just as real as the other. I do not talk as loud as you do at present, but I have something to say which is rather important for you to hear. Will you listen?"

"All right," said To-day, "shoot it off! But be quick, boil it down. I'm a bit shy on time."

"Well, then," continued the clear slow voice; "the first word I have to say is,—congratulations! You have done some very fine things. In science you are wonderful. You have reaped the field that Yesterday sowed. You have translated the discoveries of the Nineteenth Century into the convenient inventions of the Twentieth. You can fly, you can travel under water, you can talk far off, you make the rivers do your work, and the lightning illuminate your houses. You are a very clever person. I congratulate you."

"Thanks," said To-day; "I know I'm a wonder. There are no flies on me. What?"

"A few," murmured the gentle voice; "just a few slight blemishes! You talk far off, but you say nothing better than was said by wise men thousands of years ago. You travel fast, but you don't know what to do when you arrive. You have plenty of mechanical toys, but you seem no happier than the days whose only playthings were pebbles and shells. You are armed with wonderful weapons, but you use them in the same cruel, silly way in which the cave-man used his flint-headed arrow and his stone battle-axe,—to slay and to destroy. After all, you are hardly more than a grown-up baby or a learned barbarian."

"Oh, come now," cried To-day angrily, "you are drawing it rather thick. What about the great war I have just won for liberty and justice and peace? That counts for something."

"Yes, yes," said To-morrow soothingly, "that counts for a great deal. It will always stand to your credit. Somehow or other you brought together the free peoples of the world to resist the most monstrous military imperialism that has ever threatened mankind. At an awful sacrifice of blood and treasure you defeated the insane plot of the Potsdam robbers to subjugate the earth. You drove back the modern Huns. You made the vital friendship of the three great democratic peoples, Britain, France, and America, effective and victorious over fierce autocracy. That was great. There you reached the crest of the wave. But now you are sliding back into the trough. You have

forgotten the main thing for which you fought,
—Peace on earth. You have failed to bring
the criminals who plunged the world into blood
and tears, either to the seat of repentance, or
to the bar of justice. You are casting away
the victory which your sons died to win. You
are sinking back into sloth and selfishness and
greed, and making plans for a renewal of that
luxury which nearly ruined you before the war.
You are preparing the way for me to be an easy
prey for the next world-imperator with a shining sword. You are a slacker, a draft-evader
from the cause of Peace."

"Rough talk," growled To-day. "What would
you have me do?"

"I would have you wake to righteousness
and sin not," answered To-morrow. "I would
have you keep and show something of the same
spirit you had while the war was on,—the spirit
of unity and freedom and sacrifice and humanity and devotion to the cause of peace through
justice. If it was worth fighting for, is it not
worth defending? How can you defend it without power? How can you get power without
combination? You must either let the world
relapse into the old bloody welter of hatred
and violence, or else you must make a league
of free, enlightened nations pledged to reduce

war to a minimum and raise peace to a maximum. Look at your United States of America,—perhaps the best, certainly the strongest of all your nations. How nobly she answered the trumpet-call of liberty three years ago! From all her mainland States, from all her sea-girt islands, her sons trooped to her starry flag, and her daughters rallied round her Red Cross. She rose to the peak of her power. She won the admiration and confidence of the world. Where is she now? In the background, muck-raking. Her politicians, absorbed in partizan squabbles and personal animosities, are first in the talk and last in the procession. They propose to abandon their old allies and make a separate peace with Germany, stipulating only that America, who has suffered least from the German crime, should be the preferred creditor in the reparation. They refuse to let America take her right place in the partnership of nations to substitute reason and justice for greed and violence in international affairs. Do you ask what is her right place? As a leader, not as a laggard. 'America first,' is a wise motto. But you must read it right. America first, not for self alone, but for self and neighbour and God over all! America with wisdom to equal her wealth; America with fair-play to control her power; America contented with her possessions but not satisfied with herself till she has learned to make better use of them! America not only first, but foremost in the march of mankind out of the shadows of night toward the brightness of a better day!"

"That sounds good to me," said the voice of To-day, now grown stronger and more cheerful. "I get you on that. I'll come in if the ante isn't too high. What price America first? She's my best card in a doubtful suit. Dope out some pointers about America."

"Willingly," answered To-morrow, with a smooth tone that sounded like a smile. "The first bit of advice I have to give you is a small one but not without value. Persuade America, if you can, not to spoil the English language by overloading it with slang. A little is permissible, like red pepper in a sauce. But too much ruins the mixture. Nobody cares to drink Tobasco. In your speech I observe many expressions that are strange to me. To my descendants they will be absolutely unintelligible. America proposes to make all her polyglot citizens learn English. Good! But how can she do that if she herself forgets how to speak English decently? Is the world-speech to be a vulgar jargon, with a slovenly pronunciation

and an intolerable nasal accent? Spare me
that infliction, good To-day. Leave me the
rich and powerful language of King James'
Bible and Shakespeare and the masters of English, still intelligible, familiar, honoured, and
useful for human intercourse."

"Well," answered To-day reluctantly, "I'll
say that's one on me. But it's only a little
one. Cut it out for now, and get down to brass
tacks about America. What does she need
most?"

"Three things," said To-morrow, "America
needs very much at the present moment, if
she is to be a leader and helper of the world.

"First, she needs to bring some kind of reason
and consistency into her foreign and domestic
policy. If she is to pursue in her years of greatness that policy of isolation which became her
when she was small and weak, she must be
consistent in that line. She must not cry in
one breath, 'What do we care for Abroad?'
and in the next breath command Britain to
create an independent Irish Republic, or re-
buke France as a militaristic empire.

"If she is to preserve her old policy of personal liberty and home rule in local affairs, she
must not pass innumerable sumptuary laws
which attempt to regulate all the private habits

of men, such as smoking a pipe or chewing gum.
If she reveres her Constitution and wants to
keep it, she must not let it be eaten out by radical amendment-borers. If she wants a complete change of her old form of government,
she must seek it openly, argue it frankly and
fully, submit it to the public judgment, and
decide it by the voice of the whole people.
Above all she must beware of sudden impulses,
glittering phrases, hasty judgments, and violent reactions. Without reasonable consistency,
the bigger the democracy, the greater the danger.

"Second, America needs to begin to restore
a normal relation of currency and credit, to
practice economy in public and private expenses, and to cut her coat according to her
cloth. When a nation tries to live on the interest of its debts it leaves a big bill for the
next generation to pay. Before the war the
United States owed eleven dollars *per capita;*
now her national debt is two hundred and sixty-
five dollars *per capita.* The public purse holds
no more than private citizens put into it. The
faster you empty it the oftener you must fill
it. 'Let government spend,' means 'let us
pay.' Multiply the dollar and you put it out
of touch with the dinner. A penny saved is not

a penny earned if its value is cut in half; it is two cents lost. An extravagant government is as bad a risk as a spendthrift citizen. One hundred and four thousand public employees in Washington,—more than when the war was on,—impede business at your expense. No going concern can carry such overhead costs. Habits of thrift are worth more to a people than silk stockings and gramophones. Food and clothing come out of the ground, but not without industry and economy. Ever since Eden, the garden has needed to be tilled and dressed. Wild fruit is sweet, but there is not enough of it. The human race is never more than six months away from starvation. Without capital, labour cannot tide over seed-time and harvest. Without labour, capital becomes worthless, for there is nothing for it to buy. When you water your dollar you rob the poor man of his increased wages and the thrifty man of his savings. America is rich, but no wealth can stand the pace at which she is wasting on private luxury and public extravagance. Prudence, self-control, and a daily dose of common sense are the only tonics that will clear her brain and steady her feet, after the excess of war-time, for a new advance in the arts of peace.

IDEALS AND APPLICATIONS

"Third, America needs a better adjustment of the relations of labour and capital. About the details of this I confess my ignorance is as great as yours. You must start the experiments and I will try to work them out. But I beg you not to give me too much to do at once. Go slow and safe. Let the government learn how to run the Post Office before nationalising the railroads. Do not saddle me with any of the old experiments, like communism and agrarianism, that have been often tried and have always failed. The right of life is above the right of property: but unless property is protected life is hard to preserve. Invent some better machinery of arbitration that will gradually deliver the world from the destructive warfare of the strike and the lockout. But remember that enforced penalties of arbitration mean in the long run conscript labour and confiscated capital. Accept collective bargaining, for it has come to stay. But remember that a bargain implies two parties, equally responsible for keeping it. Do not abuse the labour-unions. Incorporate them. Hold them to the same account as other corporations. Change them from potent and perilous secret societies into responsible and useful bodies for mutual understanding and fair co-operation and increased production and better conditions of human life. Teach capital that labour is not only a commodity, but also a human force. Teach labour that property is not theft, but the reward of industry and thrift, the corner-stone of the home, and the roof that shelters the family. You call yourself a Christian, dear To-day. But your religion will not last unless it works between man and man, 'having the promise of the life that now is, as well as of that which is to come.' "

"I see what you mean," said the voice of To-day, thoughtfully. "Fewer laws, but wiser and more consistent: a straight policy and hew to the line: gradual advance rather than social earthquakes and volcanoes: better relations between men and nations based on a better understanding: improved machinery in civics, controlled by good-will and speeded up by efficiency. Well, you give me a hard, slow job, with no fire-works or jazz about it! Another kind of a programme would be more exciting. But I'll try, since you ask me. After all, I suppose I owe you something. I want you to think well of me when I have passed in my checks. Any more advisory demands up your sleeve?"

"Yes," answered To-morrow with his smiling serious voice, "there are two things more that I would urgently beg of you.

IDEALS AND APPLICATIONS

"First, do not expect too much of me. My name is not Millennium. It is just To-morrow. After me are coming many others of the Morrow family. Each one of them will have his own task in the world. Human nature will not change over night. There is a little twist of depravity that runs through it all. Weeds spring up of themselves, but good plants have to be cultivated. Give me a fair start and a good example, and I will carry on as far as I can for the Day-After-To-morrow.

"Second, and last, and most of all, I pray you to give me better men and women and children to work with. Clear your mind of that fatuous self-complacency which is the balm of life and the bar of progress. You have let your men fall behind your machines, more like slaves than masters. Look at your boasted America. Out of the first two million men in her selection draft more than two hundred thousand,—ten per cent,—could neither read nor write; yet all these were sovereign voters. Is democracy safe for the world on that basis? Do you want the new republic to be a dictatorship of the ignorant? Then you must not be surprised if they choose smooth-tongued rascals to lord it over them.

"What are you doing to make things better? You are paying more to your plumbers and your carpenters than to the men and women who teach your children. Not a factory is left to run itself without care for the engines. Yet a hundred thousand children of the greatest city of the world are left without teachers, because the pay is too small to keep the teachers alive. Does this mean that you care more for your machinery than for your children, more for your dead riches than for your living wealth? For Heaven's sake, To-day, be careful what you leave me! Remember that your children will be my masters.

"There is another thing that you have forgotten, dear To-day, in your race to be rich. The health of the people is a national asset. You are wise in medicine and surgery. You save many lives that would formerly have been lost. But what do you save them for,—for health and happy vigorous living? Why, then, were thirty-five per cent of the young men of America, gathered for the first selective draft, rejected as unfit for military service? That means that one of every three Americans between eighteen and thirty-five years of age was physically unsound or defective. Do you expect me to run the world with such a lot of cripples and weaklings? No, give me men who can work through an eight-hour day without fainting; women who are capable of bearing healthy children with a glad heart; children who can run and leap and dance and swim without falling to pieces. Sweep out your slums, abolish your sweat-shops, abandon your slow poisons, fight against your endemic diseases like the white plague which kills two hundred thousand people in America every year and disables millions more. You can not abolish death, but you can diminish sickness. You can promote health and vital joy. You can teach the habit of being well and the secret of growing strong. You can multiply the true wealth of mankind, which is a sane mind in a sound body.

"Above all give me men and women of sane mind. Let them be brave enough to face the real facts of life and wise enough to accept the natural and moral laws which are immutable. Teach them that two and two make four and not five, and that no plebiscite can change it. Teach them that righteousness exalteth a nation, and that the wages of sin is death, and that no man can make it otherwise by wishing or thinking so. Teach them that to live for self alone means to die slowly and forever. Teach them that they are not animal automata or puppets of Fate, but children of God, capable of immortality by his gracious gift. Teach them that good work is real worship, and noble service is true freedom, and unselfish love is the highest happiness.

"Give me more men and women who believe these things and live accordingly, dear To-day, and with their help I can be a good To-morrow. I can not make another world by putting it to the vote, but I can make this world a little better if I have enough persons of good-will to labour with me. We shall follow the star though the way be long and rough. We shall travel towards the light. We shall be glad of the day's journey and the night's rest, knowing that far away, in the fullness of time, there cometh a new heaven and a new earth, wherein dwelleth righteousness, and peace, and everlasting joy. Will you set my feet in this path and wish me well, To-day?"

"With all my heart," said the deep voice of To-day. "I give you my hopes, not my fears: my faith, not my doubts: my best, not my worst. Correct my mistakes; cast out my misdeeds, redress my wrongdoing; carry on what little I have begun well; hold fast the Ten Commandments and the Golden Rule. The Master of Life is greater than you and I. God bless you, To-morrow."